# Cake by
# the Ocean

## LORNA
## BARRETT

POOLBEG

Published 2024 by Poolbeg Press Ltd.

123 Grange Hill, Baldoyle, Dublin 13, Ireland

Email: poolbeg@poolbeg.com

A catalogue record for this book is available from the British Library.

ISBN 978-1-78199-517-4

www.poolbeg.com

# About the Author

Lorna lives in West Cork with her family and dog, Lionel. She works in banking and writes in her spare time. Lorna dreams of moving to Italy with Lionel and writing full time.

# Acknowledgements

Huge thanks to all the readers who have taken my books and their characters to their hearts.

To my children Adam, Pia and Fintan who encourage and support me in everything I do. Thank you for your unwavering love.

To Gaye Shortland who put huge efforts into turning my underdeveloped manuscript into this book today. Thank you, Gaye.

To Paula Campbell and all in Poolbeg. Thank you for your patience (which I tested at times, I know). Now four books in, thank you for taking a punt on me and fulfilling my dream to be published.

For Ned

# Chapter One

The shop was warm and cosy and there was a reassuring hum of the customers chattering at their tables. The smell of coffee permeated the air and mixed with the sweet smell of delicious tarts and pastries being baked in the tiny kitchen adjoining the café. 'Maud's' had the best coffee for miles around and the cakes and creations Maud baked were just as big an attraction. Even though the summer season was over in the tiny seaside village of Inchahowen in West Cork, the coffee shop and bakery were still doing a steady trade. The only difference was that there were occasional lulls when Maud got to sit down and she could also close her doors a little earlier in the evenings. She was constantly taking orders on the phone or from people who dropped into the shop, and forever coming up with new creations to top her most recent one. People had crazy ideas but there hadn't been one yet that Maud hadn't been able to turn into cake reality.

The shop was an eclectic mix of New York industrial and Parisien chic. Having visited in both cities and loved both, when fitting out the shop Maud couldn't help being influenced heavily by their vibes.

Growing up in the States, when she imagined her future self at thirty-five, she had imagined being a mom, doing the school run and dashing to her high-powered job somewhere in the city. Definintely not a baker and decorator of cakes in a remote village in West Cork, Ireland.

She turned around and saw a woman waiting to talk to her.

"Hey! How can I help you?" Maud asked, hoping to God it wasn't a cake request.

"I saw the cake you made for Nicola O'Carroll's little girl last week. It was stunning. I couldn't believe it when she said she got it here. In Inchahowen. No offence. I was hoping you could make one for my daughter. It's her birthday next Saturday."

"Sure. No offence taken. What do you have in mind?" Maud got her notebook out and pulled her pencil out of the messy bun on top of her head.

"Well. It will have to be pink, involve a princess and be glittery!"

"Oh, well, that goes without saying," Maud said and both women shared a little smile.

"I'd like three tiers, I think. Do you think that's too much?" the woman said.

"Not at all."

Three tiers for a child's birthday? Hell, yeah, it's too much! But Maud didn't say so. She was way too diplomatic for that. She was only providing the service, after all.

"I'll leave the rest to you, Maud. You're the expert. Whatever you do, I'm sure it will be perfect. Just make sure it's bigger than the O'Carrolls' cake. Some of the mothers will be stopping by and I want to wow them."

After the customer left, Maud added the note to her book. She closed the cover and sighed. She was concerned that this time she might have bitten off more than she could chew. She'd have to put in a lot of extra hours on top of the extra hours she had already factored in. But she would worry about that tomorrow.

The lunch rush was coming to an end and some of the tables were starting to empty. Maud and her sidekick Kate started to clear them off and ready themselves for the next onslaught.

"Was that another cake order?" Kate asked.

"Yeah, that makes it seven. Holy shit! Seven cakes for pick-up between Friday and Saturday. We almost won't have room to store them."

"You're going to need to get a bigger premises. Otherwise you'll be turning away business and I know you'd hate that," warned Kate. "I also know you're sick of me saying it but you're going to have to move or take the baking off site."

"But I don't want to move anywhere else. I keep telling you – I love that I can see the ocean out the window. I couldn't work in a bricked-up commercial unit churning out cakes like on an assembly line. I just couldn't do it."

Kate looked at her boss. She couldn't imagine Maud in a bricked-up anything, anywhere. Maud was one of the most beautiful women Kate had ever seen. Her blonde hair and big blue eyes. Her tall slim frame. Like all the residents of Inchahowen, Kate agreed that Maud was way too sophisticated for this place. But, for whatever reason, Maud loved it and wasn't budging anytime soon.

"OK, but you know I'm right. You'd do a bomb in a busy location. But if you're content making cakes for the local births, deaths and marriages, then who the hell am I to interfere?" Kate was weary of having to bring it up in conversation again.

"Let's just get the seven cakes ready for this weekend and maybe we'll talk about expanding when we're done."

Yeah, right, thought Kate. Maud's lack of ambition baffled her. With that the phone rang and she heard Maud taking another order. She caught her eye and Maud winked at her. Kate rolled her eyes to heaven. Her boss just could not say no. She would stay up all night baking and icing cakes rather than disappoint a customer.

Kate continued to clear tables, all the while imagining Maud in Cork city. Or Dublin. New York even. OK, now she was getting carried away. But Maud's talent for baking was a miracle to Kate. She felt so lucky to be learning her craft from a true master of the art. And not only were Maud's creations incredible to look at, they also tasted scrumptious. People were always shocked and surprised when the inside of the cake lived up to the promise of the outside.

"Right. That's it. Do not allow me to take one more. OK?" Maud said, returning to help Kate.

"Like I could stop you!" Kate mumbled under her breath as she put the dirty dishes in a plastic tub and took them out back to the dishwasher. She was still muttering about scaling up and expanding the business when she got back out front.

Maud put her arm around Kate. "Jeez, how did I end up working with Ireland's entrepreneur of the year? Will you remind me again, please?" she said.

She looked at Kate. Even wearing a T-shirt, jeans and an apron, she managed to look gorgeous. Her green eyes and auburn hair caused people to stop and look at her. But she acted like she was unaware of how beautiful she was. Maud felt lucky to have Kate working with her. If it wasn't for Kate, she wouldn't have been able to take on as much work as she did. And when she wasn't being a complete pain in the ass, going on about scaling up the business or moving to the city, she was also a great friend.

"Ha, yeah right. I turned my back on a life of money and success in the corporate world to bake birthday cakes for a crowd of ungrateful teenagers and their snooty parents," Kate said with mock seriousness.

In fact, Kate had left a great job in a telecom company in Dublin to come home to look after her sick father. During the time that she cared for her dad, she had plenty of time to think and she realised that although her job was financially very rewarding, it didn't feed her soul.

She began to revaluate her life and came to the realisation that she wanted to be her own boss. She wanted to run her own business. She had no idea when she moved back home that she would fall in love with the business of cake. There was no doubt that she loved to eat cake but she just never knew that she had such a passion for making it.

"But – it suits me just fine," she went on. "For now! I'm learning from you and I can keep dropping you hints about expansion and maybe, hopefully, someday you'll listen to me."

"Right!" said Maud. "For now we're going to have to forget going global and attend to the locals. Get your apron on. We're going to need a ton of cake batter."

# Chapter Two

Cake wasn't in Maud Sullivan's plans either. When she left college she worked in a fancy little art gallery in Beacon Hill in Boston. She married Ted Hamilton straight out of college, bought a house in Back Bay, close to her parents, and all in all imagined their life very differently to how it turned out.

⇢⇢⇢ ⇇⇇⇇

After four boys, Maud's arrival into the world was celebrated like that of a first child. Her parents, Hélène and James, were overjoyed. Although they, of course, loved their boys, they had always longed for a little girl. James, being Irish, thought it was the most normal thing in the world to have a large family but for Hélène, who was from Paris and an only child, homelife seemed chaotic sometimes. Maud was adored by everyone, especially her oldest brother Patrick. Patrick was ten when Maud was born and he was her protector. When boys were teasing her or pulling her hair, Patrick would appear as if out of nowhere and dare the others to lay a hand on her.

On their parent's strict instructions, her brothers walked her to and from school and minded her like she was a precious diamond.

Maud knew only love in her childhood. Their house was always full of noise and boisterousness and Maud was always at the centre of the goings-on. Her friends loved to come over to her house because of her brothers and most developed crushes on them.

Maud especially liked it when her brother Joe's friend Ted came to visit. He was a handsome football player with blond hair and green eyes and he made a big impression on the youngest Sullivan. When Maud was about thirteen she had written *"Maud loves Ted"* on her school journal in red ink surrounded by a love heart. One afternoon when Ted was over, her brother Louis got the journal and ran around the house shouting *"Maud loves Ted!"* at the top of his voice, all the while waving the journal in the air.

Maud thought she would die of mortification. She wanted to kill Louis but only after she killed herself. Her mom eventually made Louis stop and sent him to his room. But now Ted knew how she felt about him. She ran to her own bedroom and locked the door. She wouldn't come out even after Ted had gone home and she didn't eat for two days afterwards.

Every time Ted came to the house, which was much less frequently after that, she hid away. He was three years older than her and she knew he must have thought she was a baby. He seemed grown up and sophisticated and she had barely hit puberty.

Over time the embarrassing memories started to fade along with her desire to kill her brother. When Maud was eighteen, she was surprised when Ted came to her birthday party. She purposely hadn't invited him. She reckoned he wouldn't want to come and she had learned at a tender age that humiliation should and would be avoided at all costs.

Maud was hanging out with her friends, trying desperately not to look in Ted's direction. When he came over and asked her to go outside and have a beer with him, her first instinct was to say no. But she was brought up to be polite, and she heard herself accepting his offer.

"You look really pretty, Maud," he said as they walked outside the patio doors and in the direction of the bar that her brothers had set up at the end of the garden.

He was very close and she could smell his aftershave. She wished that she hadn't worn the hideous dress her mom had picked out for her. Mother and daughter almost had World War Three in the store, trying to find something suitable for the occasion. Maud wanted to wear jeans and a belly top but her mother refused outright. She ended up compromising on a light-pink knee-length dress that showed off her blossoming figure but not too much flesh. Right now she wished she had refused to wear the ridiculously expensive dress more suited to an octogenarian.

"My dress is hideous – you don't have to pretend," she said.

"No, really. You look very … mature."

Mature? Great, thought Maud. Old-fashioned and out of date is what he really meant.

"Ted, you really don't need to be kind. It's fine. I look like a geriatric. I did it for my mom. I owed her for dressing like one of the boys for the first eighteen years of my life.

"You're crazy. You look hot. Not dressing like a boy suits you," he said.

Maud felt her insides do a somersault. Did Ted just say that she looked hot? No, he couldn't have, she decided. Ted was finished law school and was working with one to the city's biggest law firms. He was just being his super-polite self. Being nice to his friend's little sister.

She felt Ted take her hand. She looked at him and she wasn't sure what it was she saw in his eyes. It didn't look like a glance between friends. There was more to it. His hand sent little shocks through her and she followed as he led her to a dimly lit part of the garden. Ted knew the Sullivans' garden like the back of his hand. The chestnut tree with the thick trunk was a great hiding place when they were kids. He pulled Maud closer as they both became invisible behind the tree. She felt Ted's lips on hers. It was a dream. The kiss felt exactly like she knew it would. Exactly like she had fantasised every day since she was a child, hopelessly in love.

"I've wanted to do that for five years. I hope you don't mind," he whispered into her ear.

"You have?" Maud was floored. Was this a joke?

"Didn't you ever notice? I always thought I acted like a dork around you."

"Why didn't you tell me?"

"What? And ruin everything? You're my best friend's sister. If you didn't feel the same way, I'd be way too embarrassed to come to your house."

"I've always felt the same way. Kiss me again and never stop."

# Chapter Three

Six years later, Maud had everything a girl could possibly want. She married Ted and they moved into their dream home. She had to pinch herself sometimes. Her dreams had become a reality.

At the beginning they cooked dinner together every evening and went out for breakfast at the weekends. Maud continued to work in the gallery. It wasn't her ideal job but it would do while she was trying to figure out what she was passionate about. She envied Ted who loved his job and had no doubts about the path he chose.

Ted's career was really taking off. He was working long hours lately due to a merger with another international law firm based in New York. He regularly left Boston on a Monday morning to go to New York, not returning until Friday. Maud was glad to see him so happy in his work but hated that it took him away from her for long periods of time.

"Will the deal be finalised soon?" she asked, hating that she sounded whiney. She was dropping him off outside the departure terminal at Logan Airport.

"Soon, baby. I'm gonna make it up to you. I know I've been distracted for months. I think we should book a vacation. Maybe Mexico. Or Puerto Rico. Somewhere hot and with no WiFi."

"Don't say it if you don't mean it. You know I'll be on to it straight away."

"If this meeting goes the way I plan on it going, this will be the last trip to New York for a long time. And, believe me, there will be nobody happier than me if that happens. I'm sick of getting on flights but if it's just me and you and that little tiny bikini of yours, I'll gladly travel. Now wish me luck," he said and he kissed her deeply before getting out of the car at the drop-down area.

*"You don't need luck! You're the best! I love you, sweetheart!"* she shouted after him as he walked into the terminal.

On the ride home Maud thought about lying on a beach with Ted. Making love in the afternoon in their cool bedroom. Still, she wouldn't book the vacation just yet. The merger had already missed several deadlines. She would wait until she heard the fat lady sing.

By way of consolation, she decided to organise a trip to Atlanta for the following weekend. Her brother Joe and his wife Pam had moved down south for Pam's job and she missed seeing them. She would call Joe later and tell him. She was sure Ted would be pleased as he had been working so hard lately. It would be just like the old days. The four of them hanging out. It was September and Atlanta should have cooled down a bit from the oppressive temperatures of high summer. The thought cheered her as she drove home through the nearly deserted streets just as the city was coming to life.

Maud showered and got dressed when she got home. The gallery didn't open until ten so she had plenty of time to get herself ready. She switched on the small TV set in the kitchen. The 24-hour news channel that Ted always watched was on. She changed channel to some rerun of an old sitcom. She then switched the TV off. She put on coffee and then changed her mind. She felt restless somehow. She reckoned she was just excited about spending the weekend with Ted and with Joe and Pam. Her phone rang and it made her jump.

"Ted?" she said, pressing the green button.

"It's Mom. Daddy is on his way over to you right now. He will be there very shortly. Don't answer the phone to anybody until he gets there. *Do you hear me?* Don't answer to anyone until Daddy gets there."

"What? Why? Mom?"

"Just do what I say, honey. Daddy is on his way so don't worry."

Maud hung up the phone. Nothing was making any sense. She turned the TV back on and switched back to the news channel. The chirpy hosts were laughing about something or other. But Maud's attention was drawn to the ticker tape running across the bottom of the screen. A plane crash. A shuttle from Boston to New York.

She felt the blood leave her extremities. She knew he was gone. She felt it in every fibre of her being. She didn't move until she heard her dad at her front door.

"Darling ..."

"He's gone, isn't he?"

Her father looked like he would have rathered it was him on the plane.

"Yes, sweetheart. I'm so sorry."

A part of Maud died the day Ted was killed. The horror and the pain of losing the person she loved most was almost unbearable. She grieved for Ted. She grieved for the children they planned and so badly wanted. She grieved for a future that was now not to be.

# Chapter Four

James and Hélène urged Maud to move home to live with them but Maud staunchly refused to leave the home she shared with Ted. She didn't go to work. She didn't get dressed most days. Her family rallied around her but Maud could barely feel their presence. She wanted Ted. Only him. She let people drift in and out of her house without engaging with any of them.

She couldn't sleep at night. She sometimes nodded off during the day but these catnaps didn't make up for the sleep she was missing out on. She was prescribed sleeping tablets but wouldn't take them. She was afraid she would become dependent on them.

One night in the weeks after Ted's death she lay in bed, wide awake as usual. She stared at  Ted's wardrobe and imagined that the clothes were moving by themselves, that Ted had taken up residence in one of his old suits. A part of her realised how crazy that was. She got up out of bed and put on her dressing gown. It was two in the morning. She got in her car and started to drive.

She showed up at her parents' front door.

"I ... I can't ..." she sobbed.

"I know, my darling. Come in. We'll take care of you," Hélène said, taking Maud's hand and leading her inside.

Maud let Hélène tuck her into her old bed in her childhood bedroom. Hélène held her daughter's hand.

"I'll wait until you fall asleep," she whispered to Maud.

"You'll have a long wait, Mom. I don't sleep."

"Well, then, I'll stay here with you all night."

Maud heard her mom nod off some time later but the solace of sleep still evaded her. Her mom's presence did give her comfort though and she felt less strung out with her hand holding hers.

❧ ❧

Maud still spent her days in her dressing gown, unable to muster up the desire or the energy to get herself dressed. She let her mother bathe her and wash her hair. She used to sit in the warm soapy water with her knees pulled up to her chin and feel her mom's hands massaging her scalp.

It made her feel safe. It made her feel like a child again.

Hélène hoped that it wouldn't come to where she had to spoon-feed Maud. She had no interest in food whatsoever and she was fading away before their eyes.

Hélène and James were beside themselves with worry and tried to get Maud some help. Her doctor prescribed some pills but Maud wouldn't take them. Like with the sleeping tablets, she was afraid that if she started she wouldn't be able to stop.

She was in limbo. She felt neither alive nor dead. She had no great desire to leave the world but she wasn't sure there was enough left to anchor her to it.

"I'm going to Mémère," Maud said out of the blue one day, using the pet name for her French grandmother.

"*Certainment.* I will go with you," said Hélène, shocked by her daughter's announcement. "A vacation is just what you need. What we both need."

"No, Mom. I want to go on my own. I've made you and Dad miserable enough for long enough. I think it's somebody else's turn," she said with a half-smile.

Maud would be eternally grateful to her parents and hoped that some day she would be able to repay them for being exactly the people she needed them to be at this time.

"We are sad for you," said Hélène. "We loved Ted too and we miss him. He was like one of our boys."

"I know, Mom. But I'm not making things any better by spending my days crying and moping around the house. I've already ruined Thanksgiving. At least you might have some chance of having a Christmas where everybody doesn't end up puffy-eyed from crying."

James drove Maud to Logan Airport. He was conscious that the last time his daughter was at the airport it was when she waved Ted off on his last journey. James sat with her while she waited to board her flight. He put his arm gently over her shoulder and she leaned into him. They made some small talk about her brothers and their families. About how Patrick, Hugo, Louis and Joe were doing and who would be coming back to Boston for Christmas. James didn't want to put any pressure on her but he told her that he and Hélène would miss her being there.

"Joe and Pam are flying in from Atlanta. They are going to stay with Pam's parents but come to us for dinner. It will be a tough time for all of us," and he gave her shoulders a squeeze.

"Daddy, I don't know how I could face it. Them. Any of it. I just feel so sad. It doesn't seem right to celebrate."

"Life goes on, darling, life goes on. Cruel as it may be, it's the way it is."

"I'd better go now. The lines for security will probably be crazy."

"I'll miss you, sweetheart. It was wonderful to have you home with us. Even if the circumstances were so tragic."

"You and Mom saved my life, Dad. I don't think that's an exaggeration."

James almost cried. He would do anything for her. And the thought of anything happening to his only daughter scared the life out of him.

"You saved yourself, girleen. You're a lot stronger than you know. Now safe journey. *Go n'éiri an bothar leat*," he said, giving her his usual Irish blessing.

"Bye, Daddy – kiss Mom for me."

Maud stepped into the line for security and patiently waited for the line to move. The lines moved at a snail's pace as people removed shoes and belts and looked surprised as the security staff instructed them to put liquids into clear plastic bags. Maud found herself getting annoyed by the length of time it was taking to get to through. It had been twenty years since 9/11. Surely everybody in the world knew about the liquids rule at this stage. She found herself getting impatient to get on the plane. Nothing would bring Ted back. He was gone but she was still here. She owed it to herself to find a reason to live again and Paris would be the first stop on her quest.

# Chapter Five

Maud's grandmother, Marielle, lived in a tiny mezzanine apartment on the Rue de Rouen on Ile St. Louis. Maud took the train from Charles de Gaulle and then a taxi to her grandmother's little apartment. She used the key Hélène had given her for the door on the street and stepped into the interior courtyard.

Each time Maud visited, which wasn't much since she had started college, she was struck by how magical this place was. She took the windy stairs up to the apartment on the first floor.

Mémère's door was open. *Is the woman crazy?* Maud thought. Leaving her door in the middle of Paris wide open? Marielle thought she still lived in a time where you could do that and not run the risk of being robbed or killed.

"*Mémère, I'm here!*" she called, walking through the hallway into the tiny kitchenette.

"*Ma petite chérie! Ma pauvre, petite chérie!*"

Marielle took her granddaughter in her arms.

Mémère seemed to get smaller every time Maud saw her.

"It's so good to be here, Mémère. Thank you for letting me come. It's so lovely to see you!" She hugged her tiny little grandmother and thought she'd break her, she was so fragile. She thought of the door and an intruder snapping her like a twig. "You know you should keep your door locked!"

"Who is going to come in here, *huh*?" Marielle protested. "You cannot get into the courtyard without a key so what can happen to me? *As-tu faim?*"

"*Non, merci.*" Still, Maud was never hungry these days. She had played with the food on the plane but barely ate anything.

"You go to your room now. Settle yourself in. Perhaps get some sleep," Marielle said. "I will wake you when dinner is ready."

Maud was about to tell her grandmother that she didn't sleep either but Marielle had already disappeared into the tiny kitchen.

Maud knew eating and sleeping were crucial for a healthy life but no matter how hard she tried, both remained elusive.

Maud looked around the little apartment. It had been years since she'd been here. She had visited Paris with Ted but they had stayed in a fancy hotel off the Champs-Élysées. She remembered visits with her mom when she was a child. A child with not a care in the world.

She climbed the steps to the mezzanine with her bag and set it down on the floor. She would unpack later. She sat down on the bed and looked up at the ceiling. She had made the move to Paris, but would it make anything better? She was still a basket case. Only now she was a basket case in France.

She felt weary all of a sudden. It had been fourteen hours since she had left her parents' house. She lay down on the bed and put her head on the pillow. She kicked off her shoes which thudded onto the wooden floor.

She closed her eyes and tried to concentrate on her breath, just like the therapist had shown her. She was getting better at it. When her mind started to wander, she managed to pull herself back to her body. Feeling herself breathe in through her nose. Feeling the air fill her lungs. Fill her stomach. Holding. Then the exhale. Deflating her lungs until she felt like an empty vessel. *Breathing in. Breathing out. Breathing in. Breathing out. In. Out. In. Out.*

⤜⤜⤜ ⤛⤛⤛

Maud nearly hit the roof. Literally. The ceiling was only a few feet above her bed.

"What the f ... Oh, Mémère. What? Is dinner ready?"

"Dinner? No, no, *ma petite.* It's morning. You missed dinner completely," her grandmother said, gently kissing her on the forehead.

"What? No, it can't be. I don't sleep. I mean, I haven't slept a full night since ... well, since . . ."

"I checked you several times last night and you were very definitely asleep."

A whole night! Maud couldn't believe it. Since Ted died, the most she slept without a sleeping pill was twenty minutes. She almost cried with relief. She had felt that she would never have a peaceful night's sleep again in her life. But she had. It could be done.

"Come," said her grandmother. "We will have some coffee and we will talk. It has been too long since I've seen my favourite granddaughter."

Maud smiled. She was her only granddaughter, Hélène being an only child. She watched her grandmother walk down the stairs and then swung her legs out of bed. She had imagined it would take her days to feel right after arriving in Paris what with the time difference and jet lag, but she was surprised at how rested she felt. She was still in the clothes she had travelled in and knew that she would be doing everyone a favour by showering. She got her toilet bag and a change of clothes from her case and headed downstairs, shouting to Marielle in the kitchen that she was going to take a shower.

When she emerged from the bathroom, clean and wearing fresh clothes, she joined her grandmother at the table where two cups of coffee sat.

"So, *ma petite*? How are you? And don't say fine. I want to know the truth."

"I don't know how I am, Mémère," Maud said honestly. "I'm coping a bit better as the weeks go by. I only think of Ted every minute now instead of every second."

Her grandmother took Maud's hand and squeezed it.

"I had to get out of Boston, you know. Too many memories. And poor Mom and Dad. I've put them through so much heartache. I've brought my sadness to their door and made it theirs. I don't know how they put up with me. You know what our house is usually like. Full of noise and laughter. But lately you could hear a pin drop. It's like everybody's afraid to breathe."

"They love you. They do not just put up with you, as you think. They want you to find happiness again. You will see, *ma chérie*, things will get better. The sad times will pass. Good times will come again. Everything is temporary. Even this terrible pain you are feeling now."

Maud hoped her wise old grandmother was right. In the immediate aftermath of the airplane crash, she had felt nothing. But now the nothings were slowly being replaced by small somethings. Like the instinct to come to Paris. Knowing that she had to get out of Boston and leave the comfort of her parents and her old home. Being in Paris felt like it was of someone else's doing. She could hardly believe that she had been the one to instigate the trip. Not only that, she had slept the night and felt hunger pangs in her tummy.

While her grandmother made another pot of coffee, Maud let herself out of the apartment and into the street. She walked around the corner to the boulangerie. The same one that she and her brothers had been despatched to when they were children on their visits with their mother. She stepped inside and her nostrils were tantalised with the wonderful aromas of freshly baked bread and cakes. The smells brought back memories of the five of them, she herself barely tall enough to see over the counter. The place hadn't changed a bit in the intervening decades.

The smell almost made her forget that she was sad or broken. She picked out a rustic loaf and some croissants. The boulanger wrapped them in brown paper and handed them to her. She paid him, thanked him and left the shop.

She took her time going back to the apartment and looked in the windows of the stores which were yet to open. She had always been besotted with Paris. She never felt like a tourist in the City of Light. She had the skinny on all the best places to eat. The best coffee. The best boulangeries. She had spent summers following Hélène and Marielle around and there was nothing those two ladies didn't know.

Marielle was in the kitchen brewing some coffee when Maud got back. The smell in the apartment was a mix of last night's missed dinner of beef and onions and this morning's coffee.

Maud went to the lounge and opened the windows to the balcony. She stuck her head out of the glass doors. She took a deep breath in. It seemed like all Paris was baking a loaf. Food was having a very strange effect on her senses, she noticed.

"Who will eat all that bread, *chérie*?"

"I will, Mémère. I'll eat the croissants too. There's one there for you."

"I do not eat bread. How do you think I keep my figure? But you, *ma chérie*, you need to eat. You are so thin. And Frenchwomen rarely say somebody is too thin, you know."

Maud had to admit that her grandmother sure looked good for almost eighty years of age. Hélène was in her fifties and she looked pretty good too. Maud hoped that she had inherited these women's genes.

"That's good because I feel like I'm going to eat myself better. God, that bakery this morning. It actually put a smile on my face. I couldn't help it. I forgot all about how miserable I am when I was in there among all those breads and pâtisseries. Everyone in there looked pretty happy too, come to think of it."

"Food can make you very happy, *chérie*, but it can also make you very sad if you no longer fit into your clothes."

"Well, hopefully I will be able to control myself before it all gets out of hand," Maud said, breaking off a big chunk of bread and spreading it with a soft cheese she'd found in the fridge.

Marielle was delighted to see that Maud had a bit more life in her than when she had arrived the night before. There was definitely more pep in her step and a bit of the Irish glint in her eyes.

⤞⤞ ⤝⤝

Maud and Marielle went out for a walk after breakfast. The air was crisp and the city mostly belonged once again to the Parisiens. There were still lots of tourists but not as many as clogged every street in the summertime.

Maud felt a small shift in her. She felt lighter in herself somehow. She had got used to carrying the weight of her grief, feeling it slowly crush her. She relished being away from Boston and the memories of Ted everywhere she looked.

Marielle stopped outside the butcher's. "I want to get something for dinner," she said.

"No. Let's eat out tonight. You pick the restaurant," Maud replied.

"We can eat at home, *chérie*."

"We can but we're not going to. Not tonight or any other night for that matter. We are going on a quest to find the best food in Paris."

For the first time in a long time, she laughed. She put her arm through her grandmother's and they walked home.

# Chapter Six

The quest for the perfect meal continued night after night. They were on a mission to find the best restaurant in Paris and it was taking a long time. Maud didn't know how long more she could do this to Marielle. Her poor grandmother had complained to Maud that morning that her skirt would not close properly on her. Maud had noticed that her own jeans seemed to be quite snug on her these days too. There was also a slight muffin top appearing above her waist.

Along with her expanding waistline was an expanding love of food. Maud had discovered a passion for food she never knew she had. Food. Simple as that. She loved food. She loved how it made her feel. She loved that the smell of fresh bread baking could instantly cheer her up. She didn't know anything else that could have that same effect. She was falling in love with everything associated with food. She was fascinated by chefs and restaurants and spent her time in them, absorbing every bit of information she could.

She made a decision. She was going to become a baker right here in the French capital.

Marielle encouraged her granddaughter's newfound passion and she and Maud looked up possible places for Maud to learn. Marielle suggested Le Cordon Bleu but Maud swatted the notion away.

"I couldn't apply for Le Cordon Bleu," she said.

"Whyever not?" asked Marielle.

"It's . . . well, it's such an iconic school. I'm sure they only take the best."

"And that is exactly why you should go there."

"Do you think I have a chance of getting in? Seriously?"

"Certainment. You know more than any chef knows at this stage."

Maud googled Le Cordon Bleu on her phone. There seemed to be a constant intake of students for various courses of varying lengths. The application form could be filled out online. She started to fill in the form. She had to attach a letter outlining the reasons why she wanted to be admitted to arguably the best cookery school in Europe. She could hardly articulate what it was that had got hold of her since she arrived in Paris but she wrote the letter from her heart. She was shocked when a week later she got a letter addressed to her grandmother's apartment in Ile St. Louis inviting her to attend the school for an interview.

⋙ ⋘

Maud arrived at 8 Rue Leon Delhomme, fifteen minutes early for her interview. She felt very privileged to have the opportunity to apply for such a school. It seemed like the rest of her life depended on her being accepted. She was more nervous than she had ever been before in her life. Her palms were sweating as she sat there twirling her résumé in her hands.

"*Vous pouvez entrer maintenant,*" the gentleman behind the desk told her.

"*Merci,*" she said and straightened her skirt and then her shoulders.

She walked into a room that wouldn't have looked out of place in Versailles. She was slightly intimidated by the men behind the desk at the top of the room and was self-conscious as she walked what seemed like a mile to get to the chair placed in front of them.

She took her seat and suddenly felt all of her nerves leave her. She saw Ted's face in front of her. He winked at her and she saw his beautiful smile. He told her to breathe, to be calm. He told her she was going to be great. And somehow she believed him.

The interview was tough. It was conducted in French and she hoped that nothing was lost in translation. She thought it went well but she would have to wait for at least a week to hear from them again. They told her they would write to her when they had made their decision. *Hello, twenty-first century,* she wanted to scream! She had thought letterwriting was a thing of the past. Not here in Paris obviously. Not in Le Cordon Bleu. Maud left knowing she had done everything she could to get a place on the course and now it was in the lap of the gods. Or in the lap of the three chefs who interviewed her at least.

Maud spent a nervous week waiting for the letter in the post. Marielle was glad to see that Maud's appetite was waning slightly. She was alarmed by all the food she was consuming. She was on the verge of calling Hélène to warn her that Maud was overeating and would surely have to go on a diet.

It seemed as soon as Maud focused her mind on getting a place in Le Cordon Bleu, her appetite for getting on the course surpassed her appetite for food.

The long-awaited letter arrived and Maud was shaking so much she couldn't open it. She handed it to her grandmother and watched as Marielle opened it and jumped up and down with excitement in a manner astonishing for a seventy-eight-year-old woman.

"Your *maman* and *papa* will be so happy, *chérie*," Marielle said, hugging Maud tightly.

"Yeah, I think they will be. I didn't tell them anything about it. I'll call them now."

"No need. I've been keeping them up to date on everything. They knew about the interview and like me they knew that you would get in. They wanted to be here to celebrate with you so they're arriving in Paris later tonight!"

⟫⟫⟫ ⟪⟪⟪

There were many times when James and Hélène had despaired of ever seeing the old Maud again. When Maud and Marielle met them in the hotel lobby, they hardly recognised their little girl. She was animated and definitely healthier than she had been when she left Boston three months before.

"You look wonderful, darling," said Hélène, hugging her tightly.

"You do. You look marvellous," said James, taking his turn to hug her.

"Paris and Mémère have done wonders for me," said Maud. She immediately felt terrible. Her parents couldn't have done more for her after Ted's death. They were incredible. "I didn't mean that you didn't ... I didn't ..."

"You don't have to explain anything, sweetheart. You've got a sparkle back in your eyes and you're about to embark on a new adventure. You're a survivor and we're so proud of you," James said.

She had survived. Something terrible had threatened to take her down but she fought it with ammunition from an arsenal she didn't know she had. Yes, she was a survivor. She took her parents by the arms and walked to the restaurant where she had made dinner reservations.

Marielle had cried off. Her waistline had taken a battering and she wanted to stay at home and eat an apple for dinner.

Maud and James laughed as Hélène took control of ordering dinner. The American twang she had picked up over the years in the States disappeared and you would have thought she had never left her hometown.

"I love being in Paris," she said. "I have so many lovely memories here. I'm so glad you will be studying here, chérie. I know I was against you coming here, but you proved to me that it was the best thing for you. I wanted you to stay so that I could make you better but I see it was better for you to be here with Mémère. You had to get away from home, I know that now."

"I wasn't trying to get away from you guys, you know that. I would still be crying in my room if I had stayed. What I needed was a complete change of scene. I can feel that Ted is happy for me too. Don't ask me how but I can feel his presence sometimes. Like when I was waiting to be interviewed at Le Cordon Bleu, he was telling me to take deep breaths and to calm down. He said they'd love me, that I'd do great. I really felt as if he was right there with me."

She looked away, embarrassed by her admission. Her parents would think she was losing her marbles.

"He was," said Hélène. "He always will be. Love like yours never dies, *ma petite*."

Just then the waiter came by with their first course and distracted them from their sad thoughts. Maud was glad. She had felt that her parents had suffered her pain almost as much as she had and she didn't want to drag it out any more. She wanted the mourning to stop and the living to start.

# Chapter Seven

Maud threw herself completely into her cooking. She was there at the crack of dawn and always the last to leave the kitchen. She was a bit impatient at first but soon realised that the process of becoming a qualified chef could not be rushed.

She was so eager to learn everything the chefs and professors had to teach her that she reminded herself of the nerdy kids in her class in high school. She hung on their every word and wrote down everything they put on the chalkboard into her precious notebook.

She was surprised at the mix of students at the institute. She imagined they would all be eager high-school leavers but some were considerably older than her.

She went home every evening to her little apartment and felt herself slowly but surely coming back to life. She had moved out of Marielle's apartment and, even though her grandmother protested, she was sure that she would be glad to have her apartment to herself again.

Maud wouldn't have been good company in any case. When she didn't have her nose stuck in her text books, she was trying out complex cooking methods in her tiny galley kitchen. She was happy. There were days when she didn't think about Ted for hours on end and she felt that the big black cloud that had followed her around constantly since the accident was gone.

She was able to think about him now and not break down in tears. She thought about how it would be to cook some of the wonderful culinary creations for him and how surprised he would be that she was actually able to cook at all.

⤜⤜⤜  ⤛⤛⤛

Maud graduated from Le Cordon Bleu and couldn't wait to get started on whatever was next. The problem was, she didn't know what exactly was next for her. It was winter in Paris and she didn't have a clue where she would go. She went to the institute to pick up some belongings she had left behind and looked at the notice board where jobs were posted for the graduating students.

There was a notice for a chef to join a yacht that was sailing around the Caribbean. It was freezing in Paris and the thought of the Caribbean with its crystal-clear waters and the chance to show off her newly acquired culinary skills really appealed to her.

She pulled the notice off the board so that nobody else would see it and phoned the contact number. She was hired over the phone. The yacht was sailing from Miami in a week's time. Maud couldn't believe it. She had a brand-new qualification and a brand-new job all in the space of a week.

And she had done it all by herself. She knew she had been babied and pampered all her life with decision-making always being done by someone else. She liked that she was in charge and immediately booked a transatlantic flight to Miami International Airport.

⁕⁕⁕

The flight touched down in the afternoon and Maud made her way to the marina with the directions she had been given over the phone. She found the yacht and let out a low whistle. It was enormous. She wondered just how many people she was going to have to feed on board.

She was met by Lindsey, the woman who had hired her over the phone. She introduced Maud to the rest of the crew on board. Maud was amazed at the amount of kitchen staff there were but, when she saw the standard of food they were expected to produce, she knew they would need every one of them.

Maud didn't see much of the Caribbean for the first few days. She sweated in the galley kitchen where the head chef, Chris, shouted orders at her. She spent most of her time dodging hot pans and other implements he was prone to throw at the chefs.

It was not exactly the life she had envisioned for herself when she started out on her culinary journey. She was amazed that her colleagues didn't bat an eyelid when Chris called her an idiot or questioned her credentials and ability to cook at all.

All the other chefs kept their heads down and got on with their work and Maud thought they made an effort not to make eye contact with her.

One night, after a particulary fraught exchange with Chris, Maud went up on deck to get some air. That asshole had called her a stupid fucking moron when she handed him some perfectly cooked scallops for plating. She knew they were perfect when she gave them to him but he left them under the hot lights on the line, cooking them a shade too long. She wanted to tell him to shove his goddamn job up his ass. She wanted to walk out and leave him short a cook for the rest of the trip.

Ted had left her comfortably off. So comfortable that she needn't work for the rest of her life. But she couldn't not work. With Ted gone, now more than ever she needed purpose in her life. She was out in the world on her own and there were going to be Chrises no matter where she went. She needed to learn to deal with them.

"Hey, don't take it personally," said a woman's voice behind her.

Maud turned around to see Jenna, the head waiter on the yacht.

"The guy's got major anger issues. And, lucky you, you're the new girl and you get to bear the brunt of that anger."

"I just needed to get out of there. If I stayed, I don't think I'd still have a job. Even though right now that doesn't seem like such a bad deal."

"Everybody's afraid of Chris. Afraid of upsetting the son of a bitch. Nobody says anything cos when he's on someone else's case, he's not on theirs. That's how they look at it anyhow."

Maud felt embarrassed as her body started to shudder.

"Aw, honey, don't cry," said Jenna, putting an arm around Maud's shoulders.

The gesture made Maud cry some more.

"Hey now, cut it out. If he knows he's getting to you, he'll make your life more miserable. Dry your eyes and get back down there. Don't give him the satisfaction."

"Thanks, Jenna. I was beginning to feel completely alone."

"Nah, it just takes a while. We're not bad when you get to know us. Actually we're all going out to a bar on the island when we finish later. It's a place we always go. You wanna come along?"

"Sure. I'd like that."

# Chapter Eight

After surviving the remainder of the shift from hell, Maud got ready to go out. She was glad of an opportunity to get off the boat and to get to know the people she worked with. They went to a beachside bar that looked to Maud like a shack. The bartender seemed to know them all by name. Robbie, one of the crew, ordered shots for everyone.

Maud normally didn't do shots but she didn't want to stand out as being prissy. She licked the salt off the back of her hand, knocked back the tequila and banged her glass on the bar like everyone else.

Rounds of beers followed and Maud started to enjoy herself. The crew were crazy as far as she could tell. It was obviously the endless days on the high seas that affected their mental equilibrium. A live band started up and there was an exodus for the dance floor. Maud didn't know the song and didn't join them, preferring to watch them bouncing around the dance floor from the comfort of her bar stool. She heard a voice to her left and turned around.

"You don't take that shit personally, do you, honey?" Chris said into her ear.

He was way too close for her liking and she felt some of his spittle in her ear. She wiped her ear with her sleeve as she felt his hand on her ass.

"We're not in your kitchen now so I have no problem telling you to *get your fucking hand off my ass!*"

"*Woooo!* A woman with spirit! You know, I like that, it's a real turn-on. I knew you had a little thing for Chef Chris."

"Sure I've a little thing for you. It's called pepper spray and if you don't get the hell out of my face, I'll spray it in yours!"

"Hey, hey, no need for that now! C'mon and we'll get to know each other a little bit." Chris was right up in Maud's face and she looked around for Jenna and the rest of the crew but they were pogo-ing on the dancefloor, engrossed in the music. She tried to get up and walk away but he had his arm around her waist and was pulling her back towards him.

"How 'bout you and me go outside on the beach and have a little fun? I only give a hard time to the ones I'm interested in. You and me could have some good times together before we get back to Miami."

"How 'bout you get your hands off me and leave me the hell alone? I'm not interested in having good times with anyone, especially not someone as unpleasant as you."

"Is everything alright here?" asked a man with a British accent.

"That, my friend, is none of your freakin' business," said Chris.

"Fred, hi! It's great to see you. I can't believe I've bumped into you again!" said Maud.

"You two know each other?" asked Chris.

"Intimately," said the man with the posh accent.

It was enough to send Chris trawling the bar for another victim to hit on.

When Maud was sure he was gone, she turned to the man beside her.

"Thank you so much. I'm sure he's probably harmless enough but I'm glad I didn't have to make a scene. I have to work with him for the next few weeks."

The man was maybe in his fifties, Maud reckoned. And very definitely British. He sounded like Hugh Grant. He even had the foppish fringe falling over one eye. He was still handsome but she imagined he was even moreso in his younger years.

"Oh, any time. I'm just glad I didn't have to fight him. He's a big bugger. Can I buy you a drink?"

"Oh, *em*, sure. Thanks. I'll have one of these," she said, holding up her almost empty bottle.

"So, I'll start off with the corny line. What's a nice girl like you doing in a dump like this? And I'm not trying to hit on you, by the way. Not that you're not a beautiful woman, because you certainly are. It's just that I've sworn off women. I'm Warren, by the way." He held out his hand to her.

"Nice to meet you. I'm Maud," she said, shaking the proffered hand. "I'm working on a yacht that's sailing around the Caribbean. We've been given a few days off so the crew are just letting off some steam."

"Sailing around the Caribbean, eh? That sounds like it's not the worst job in the world."

"It's not but, believe me, it's hard work. The kitchen on board is hotter than I imagine hell is. I'm not complaining though. We get to spend time on Aruba and get paid for the pleasure. It beats the hell out of winter in Paris or Boston for that matter."

"Paris or Boston? I take it from your accent you're more *'pa'k the ca'* than the City of Light."

"Yes, I'm from Boston but my mother is French. I've spent the last year with my grandmother in Paris."

"And now Aruba. You certainly get around."

"I take it from *your* accent that you're not from Aruba and that you get around too."

"I'm from London. Lived there all my life, but I realised when I got divorced that London town isn't big enough for the both myself and the ex Mrs. Hodge."

"So you and your wife didn't exactly have a harmonious parting of the ways?"

"You could say that. Anyway, let's talk about something else. Talking about Annabel brings me out in a terrible rash. Sorry, that's far too much information for having just met you."

"It's fine. You can tell me whatever you like. After all, you've just saved me from my boss, his rancid breath and his unwanted advances."

"I see you're married," he said looking at her ring finger.

"Oh. Yes. I mean, no. I'm, *em*, I'm a widow." She knew this line to be the ultimate conversation killer.

"Bugger! My big mouth. I apologise."

"You've nothing to be sorry for. It's just that I can't take off the ring. It would be like finally admitting that he's gone for good and never coming back. It's stupid, I know. Because he is gone for good. He was killed in a plane crash on his way to a meeting in New York."

Maud was surprised that she wasn't completely overcome with grief when she told Warren about Ted. She was able to talk about that September morning without shedding one tear or becoming hysterical. She could see the concern in Warren's face and she batted away his concern.

"It's fine. Let's start again and not mention our spouses. Tell me what you're doing here. In Aruba, I mean."

"Well, I suppose it began when my wife threw me out of our home. She caught me with my assistant who wasn't taking notes. You get my drift?"

"I think I do."

"Annabel had her suspicions about me and Laura. Laura made no bones about the fact that she wanted to have an affair with me and used to flirt outrageously with me at dinners, even when Annabel was there. She was a little minx. Annabel followed me to my office one morning. She saw me leave with Laura and watched us go into the Savoy. It was ten in the morning. She gave the receptionist in the hotel some cock-and-bull story about having a meeting with me and, being terribly helpful, he gave Annabel the room number. She walked in on the two of us. Naked. Well, we were naked, not Annabel. You can imagine the rest."

"I can. *Wow*. I thought that stuff only happened in movies. What did you do?"

"I jumped out of bed. Poor Laura. I didn't even think about how awful it was for her. Annabel just looked at me and then stared at my by-then redundant erection. She told Laura that she was welcome to me. She turned on her heel and left the room. She was always a classy woman. That's what I liked most about her when we met. I didn't feel much like having sex after that. I checked out and Laura went back to the office. I went home to find my clothes strewn over the street having been tossed out of our bedroom window. I was never allowed to set a foot inside my home after that."

"I suppose you deserved it."

"I did. I was an idiot. I had everything. A beautiful wife, a successful career and, most of all, two beautiful boys. But they were heady days and everybody wanted more than they already had. It was a culture that was growing in the city. I regret it but, then again, I wouldn't have ended up being a coffee plantation owner in Aruba if it hadn't been for my enormous ego."

"You've got a coffee plantation? That sounds interesting."

"I moved into an apartment after Annabel threw me out. I was miserable and I started to re-evaluate my life. I never foresaw being on my own and, now that had happened, I thought that anything was possible. The *Sunday Times* used to do a feature in their property section that compared properties in London with properties somewhere else in the world. It showed a two-bed apartment in Notting Hill for over a million pounds and a coffee plantation for a fraction of the price. The plantation came with a house and a ready-made work force. I rang the agent on Monday morning. I resigned from my job the following Friday. And here I am. The rest is history."

"*Wow!* That was a brave move. What did you do in London? Was it related to the coffee business?"

"I was a barrister. I never even drank coffee. I'm a tea man. Was a tea man. Now I drink mostly Scotch," he said, indicating the glass in his hand.

"So. Are you actually producing coffee? Did you make a go of it?"

"Of course I did. And yes, I, we, at the Five Islands Coffee Plantation are the biggest producer on the island. I'll have you know it's probably the best coffee in the world."

"Says the guy who drinks tea and Scotch," laughed Maud.

"I'm a taster. I taste the beans at a very early stage in the process. Long before some young Wall Street banker's drinking it out of his paper cup."

"I'd love to see it. Will you show me?"

"Certainly. I'd like that. I'll pick you up at ten in the morning."

# Chapter Nine

Warren beeped the horn at ten the following morning, and Maud hopped into his two-seater jeep. It looked like something left over from a war but she soon realised it was exactly what was needed to negotiate the bumpy off-road terrain where he was taking her.

He drove her to places she imagined most tourists never saw. She was taken aback by what lay outside the main tourist spots. Tourists never saw the real people who lived on the island and how dire some of their living circumstances were.

"Who lives in those shacks?" she asked.

"The workers mainly," sighed Warren.

"But how? Pretty much everyone I know is addicted to coffee and we pay five dollars for a cup of the stuff. I imagined it must be like living in the Gold Rush where everyone got rich on the back of it." She couldn't help but be shocked by the unfairness of it all. Working in scorching heat, doing back-breaking work should be rewarded financially.

"The worker is the bottom of the chain. We as producers are next. The big money goes to the corporations. They pay for the marketing, the advertising. Very little of your five dollars trickles down to the guys in the fields."

They finally reached their destination. A big sign over a huge pair of rickety gates announced that they had arrived at the Five Islands Plantation. In they went and pulled up at small building he said was his office. Ever the gentleman, he ran around the car and opened the door for Maud. He was immediately surrounded by a group of what looked like office workers, all looking for his approval or signature on documents. She watched as he discussed a problem with the roasters with one employee and an issue with the staff toilets with another.

"Sorry about that," he said as he returned to her side. "Right, let's show you around."

Maud followed Warren like a shadow for the next few hours. He showed her red berries growing on the bushes that she couldn't believe would one day be somebody's morning cup of coffee. She realised that she didn't have the first idea about the bean even though she didn't go a day without having a cup. She tasted beans which were so bitter she couldn't imagine them ever making it into her Americano.

They were soon back where they started and Warren was surrounded again by his office staff. He tossed the keys at Maud and she let herself into the jeep. She fanned herself in the heat and waited for him to finish his business. Five minutes later, he hopped into the jeep beside her. They rattled along the dirt roads back to town.

When they got to the boat, Maud turned to him.

"Warren. Surely something could be done to improve the living conditions for the workers?"

"Sure there is. We would have to get more money per tonne for the coffee we're producing."

"Do you mind me asking if you're making money."

"Some. And every cent goes back into the company."

"Oh, I'm sorry. I didn't mean to imply that you're making off with the profits."

"We're not getting a good enough price for the quality of the coffee we're producing," Warren explained to her. "We're one of the few producers who take obligations to the environment seriously. Our water treatment plant costs almost as much to run as the plantation itself."

"Why don't all the producers get together into a sort of a co-operative movement? You could advertise your green credentials. Then you could demand more surely?"

"Most of the people here don't trust me because I'm British. They don't tend to trust outsiders at all so it would be quite difficult for me to get any cooperative movement together. Also, there's a big problem with corruption here. It's hard, no, impossible to get anything done. The farmers are caught in a cycle of poor education and being kept ignorant by the government. I don't see it happening anytime soon. Look, don't lose sleep over something you can't do anything about."

Maud was distressed by his answer. She couln't accept that nothing could be done.

"Look, how about you let me take you out to dinner this evening? If you're free, that is."

"Sure. That would be lovely."

Warren picked her up in the evening. He was dressed in a suit with an open-necked shirt and Maud was flattered that he had made such an effort. It was still hot and he quickly discarded the jacket. She hopped into his jeep and they drove to the restaurant which he raved about the whole way there.

He was like someone from a different era and Maud liked it. The dinner was amazing, just as Warren had said it would be. The restaurant looked like nothing from the road but it opened up onto the water and the fish tasted so fresh that Maud imagined it had been caught right there on the beach just before they arrived.

Warren's company was as good as earlier if not better. He was knowledgeable about lots of things and Maud found herself listening to his stories with rapt attention. He told her about the cases he had argued in court and she had to really try to imagine him in his wig and gown in the courtroom. The Warren having dinner with her was tanned and relaxed and must be completely different from the barrister he used to be.

"Do you miss it? London? The bar?" she asked.

"Not any of it. This is the best move I ever made. I could very easily have stayed in London arguing for the guilty and the innocent for the rest of my days but I'm jolly glad I didn't. I do miss my sons terribly, though. They visit but not as often as I would like. I know Annabel says terrible things to them about me. When they arrive here first, things feel a little frosty. It takes a few days for them to thaw out a little bit. By the end we're all chums and they don't want to leave. Bloody awful but what can you do?"

"Have you met anybody since your wife? Since Annabel?" she asked.

"Not until now," he said, looking into her eyes.

Maud was uneasy. What was this? Was it going to be a thing? Was she ready? It had been over a year since Ted was killed. Warren was warm and funny and she couldn't help but feel relaxed in his company. She decided not to think about it and to let whatever was going to happen, happen.

When he took her hand after dinner and led her to his jeep, she let him take her back to his place.

"Would you like a drink?" he asked, tidying away a few stray items as he went towards the living room.

"Sure, whatever you're having, thanks," she said, following him.

He had a nice house which was situated right on a beach. Maud imagined most people dreamed of living some place like it. There were comfortable sofas and chairs and each one invited you to lose yourself in it. Maud opened the big sliding door and found herself on a wooden deck. She couldn't see the sea but she could hear the waves lapping on the shore and she could smell the salt in her nostrils.

Warren must have flicked a switch because a string of lights lit up the outside area. *Wow*, she thought. No wonder he loved living in Aruba. She couldn't imagine any part of London comparing to this.

She heard him approach from the living room. He handed her a glass of rum with ice and she felt it burn as it travelled down her throat. *Whoa*, neat rum. She'd better stick to just the one. They leaned together against the rail of the deck and looked at the lights of the nearby town. She felt his closeness and had a distinct feeling that something was going to happen between them.

Warren turned to her and took her glass out of her hand and put his mouth on hers. His kiss was different to Ted's. His mouth was rough and stubbly but it felt good to be kissed again. She hadn't thought she'd ever want to feel someone else's mouth on hers but she liked it.

She argued back and forth in her head for a time. She wanted this. She wanted someone to make love to her. She wanted to feel the kind of alive that only sex can make you feel. She let herself go.

Warren took her hand and led her into his bedroom. The room didn't say anything about him. It was cool with white walls and white bed sheets. A stripy chair was strewn with the clothes he wore earlier that day. The french doors were open and the muslin curtain blew in the breeze. She tried to concentrate on what was happening in the moment. She wasn't betraying Ted. He'd want her to move on, to be desired, to be made love to. Wouldn't he? *Fuck!* Her mind was full of Ted. She turned around and almost expected Ted to be the one who was holding her hand.

"I'm sorry. I ... I can't. I ..."

"Oh, my dear. Please don't apologise. Oh my goodness, don't get upset," he said, pulling a tissue from the box on his dresser. "I'm terribly sorry. I misread the situation completely."

"No. It's me. I thought I wanted to ... But it's just that I keep seeing his face. Ted. My husband. I ... I just can't do it."

"Say not another word, my dear. I'm afraid I can't drive you back to town though. I knocked back two large rums to steady my nerves. I can call you a taxi or you can stay in my guest room."

※※ ※※

The next morning, Maud woke up to the sound of the waves from the comfy bed. She pulled the sheet over her head. She was dreading having to see him. She felt like a tease. She had given him all the signals. She went back to his place knowing where it was most likely going to lead.

A knock at the door jolted her out of her thoughts.

"Tea for madam," she heard from outside.

"*Em*, yes, please," she heard herself say although she wished she was a hundred miles away.

Warren entered the room like a maitre d' with a tray held aloft. He put it down on the night table beside the bed. There was a silver teapot and china cup and saucer. A milk jug and sugar lumps in a bowl, all matching. A slice of toast and a little dish with marmalade in it. It was very British and almost made Maud laugh despite the awkward situation.

"Warren, this is lovely. But there was no need. A mug of coffee is my usual breakfast."

"Nonsense! Anyway, I want to make up for completely misreading the situation last night. It was unforgiveable of me. And to think that a beautiful young woman would be interested in an old codger such as myself is just ridiculous in hindsight."

"You're not an old codger. You're a very handsome man, And you didn't misread the signals, Warren. It's my fault. I thought I was ready to move on but I'm not."

"That's jolly decent of you, Maud. I like you. As a person, I mean. You're beautiful, intelligent and empathetic. It's not a combination I've come across a lot on this island. I would hope we can be friends."

"I'd like that," Maud said, taking a sip of her tea.

⤞⤟ ⤝⤜

Maud was glad that the yacht was staying moored in Aruba for another couple of days as it gave her more time to spend with Warren. She decided that she could do with a friend like him. He was wise and kind and she enjoyed his company.

She talked about the coffee plantation so much that Warren offered to take her to work with him the following day. She followed him around the lines of bushes and tried to learn a bit more about the business. The money Ted had left her was burning a hole in her pocket and an idea had started to form in her mind.

That night after they had eaten dinner which they cooked together she handed him some sheets of paper that were stapled together.

"What's this?"

"It's a proposal. I want to do something to challenge myself and I think I've hit on something that would benefit the two of us."

53

❧❧❧ ❧❧❧

Maud had proposed that Warren supply the coffee from his farm to her for a fairer price than he was receiving currently. He would be exclusive to her and she could charge a higher price at her end due to its quality and the provenance of the coffee.

She would open coffee houses in Boston where she would sell the coffee along with her patisseries. She would be able to vouch for the provenance of each and every bean and even have pictures of the workers on the walls of the coffee house. A large percentage of their profits would be invested back in the island in the farm's irrigation systems, the farmers and in education of the children of the workers.

She had included every last detail in the proposal and by the time Warren got to the end of the document he had a new business partner.

# Chapter Ten

Maud arrived back in Miami and said her goodbyes to the crew. On the flight to Boston, she reflected on her cruise around the Caribbean. It may have sounded like a dream job but the work was harder than she anticipated: the heat in the galley kitchen, the egos she had to deal with, barely seeing daylight for days on end. On balance she was glad she had taken the job, but she knew she would never do it again. Anyway, she had a new business to develop. And she could not wait to get going.

James and Hélène were thrilled to see Maud and even more thrilled to see their girl had her spark back. She was unrecognisable from the shell she had become after Ted's death.

"So, it looks like the last few months have done you the world of good," said James.

"It did. I finally got something to give my life some meaning again."

Maud filled her parents in on the encounter with Warren and the Five Islands Coffee Plantation. They knew nothing about the coffee industry but couldn't deny that it had given Maud her joie de vivre back.

She got to work straight away, looking for the perfect location to open her first CaraBean coffee shop.

She trawled the city with estate agents, turning one premises down after another. Every place she looked at some good points but they just didn't tick every single box. She was walking through Faneuil Hall and passed the coffee shop that she had worked in while she was in senior year in High School. It was closed down and there was a number for a letting agent on a huge hoarding above the door.

She knew it was perfect. She knew the kind of people who passed the door every day would love what she was doing and appreciate the integrity of the product. She called the agent and asked him to meet her there straight away.

Maud didn't want to waste any time so she told him that she would pay the asking price plus ten per cent but she had to have an answer by the close of business. She went home and sat on her hands. Hélène worried that she would have a nervous breakdown if she didn't get the shop. The phone finally rang with the agent giving her the good news. The lease was hers. CaraBean was born.

She set up shop, sparing no expense. Her shop had little wooden carts out front with mini-sacks of coffee beans and the inside was decorated with photographs of the farmers and children who lived on the Five Islands Coffee Plantation. In her advertising she put a big emphasis on the fact that it was Fair Trade, environmentally compassionate coffee and that a percentage of the profits were going back into the local community where it came from, to help with education and improving living conditions.

This combined with her delicious tarts and pastries made CaraBean a must-go-to destination in the city. The *Boston Globe* did a feature on her and the company's ethos and business really started to boom. Soon Maud opened a second shop in the financial district and then another and another. She asked her brother Patrick to join her in the business as it was all getting too big for her to handle on her own and he was a natural business brain.

⁘⁘⁘

Within three years there were sixty CaraBean shops in the US and the number increased to eighty within five years. They had expansion plans to move outside the US into Canada and Europe. The shops outside the original shop in Faneuil Hall were all franchised with each franchisee being educated on the ethos of the organisation.

Maud was astounded by its success and relieved that Patrick had given up his position at his law firm where he was partner. Going to work together was like an extension of when they were kids. They worked hard but also had a lot of fun at it.

They were now both wealthy beyond anything they ever dreamed of and Warren was also doing very nicely out of their business relationship. He had increased productivity and had bought another holding. He grumbled occasionally to Maud that he only wanted to grow beans as a hobby and was busier now than he had been in London.

She asked if he wanted out but he didn't. He couldn't. His sons were spending more time with him and wanted to leave England and join him on the island and get involved in the business too. He had managed to cobble together a sort of cooperative movement and slowly but surely the money was starting to filter back to the farmers and the community.

Maud spent every holiday season with Warren in the Caribbean. They sometimes stayed at his house but sometimes travelled to other islands. She worked so hard for the rest of the year that she always looked forward to some downtime with Warren. He was still as good company as ever and had become an expert in all things coffee. Maud sometimes felt guilty for turning what was to be a retirement hobby for Warren into an enormous enterprise that took all his time.

"It's probably a good thing," he said. "I'd most likely have drunk myself to death at this stage if I didn't have it. And my boys are here with me now so I'll never complain about it."

This made Maud feel better about things. The success of the venture had taken them all by surprise.

⤜⤜⤜⤜ ⟪⟪⟪⟪

The following Christmas, Warren surprised her by saying he wanted to spend the holidays in England. He said his heart suddenly ached for the cold and misery of an English Yuletide. He extended an invitation to Maud but she reckoned that if she was to spend the holidays in the cold, it should be in Boston with her own family.

Patrick had been trying to persuade her to stay at home and experience the magic of the holidays with the children ever since Ted died. He alway lost out to Aruba so was delighted at the thought of all of the siblings being together at Christmas again.

The day was chaotic and went by in a blur of eggnog and mountains of wrapping paper. Maud's mom made the day as special as she had done when they were all children and they all ate and drank more than they should have.

The children kept the adults amused all day with their toys and antics. Once Christmas night came, Patrick and Martha were packing up the kids and the ridiculous amount of presents they had been given. Maud had planned to stay with her parents but at the last minute decided she would go home to her apartment. She asked Patrick to drop her off on his way home. Hélène tried to persuade Maud to stay, saying her room was made up and ready for her but Maud wanted to wake up in her own bed in the morning. She said goodnight to her parents and thanked them for a wonderful Christmas.

"You OK, sis?" Patrick asked as he got out of the car to walk her to her door.

"Sure, I just overdid it on the booze. I'll pay for it tomorrow. I'd rather have a hangover alone than have Mom trying to feed me a mountain of food in the morning. It was a great day."

"Sure was."

"I love you so much, Patch," she said, using her childhood name for him. "Night, you guys! Safe home!" she said and blew kisses at Martha and her niece and nephew in the back of the car.

⟶⟫⟫ ⟪⟪⟵

Maud's house was as warm as toast and she got into her PJs. She thought about the day and vowed to spend every Christmas from now on with her family. They'd had such a great time and she felt so loved by them all. She brushed her teeth and got into bed. She was asleep almost before her head hit the pillow.

When the phone rang she felt like she had been asleep for hours. She looked at the time on her phone and reaslised it was only past two. Her brother Louis was on the other end of the phone. She was confused. He told her she had to get to Mass General right away.

"What? Louis? What's going on?"

"It's Patrick. Just get here. *Now*."

Filled with dread, she rushed out into the cold still wearing her PJs with her winter coat over them. She drove the empty streets and abandoned the car outside the hospital entrance. When she got inside the hospital, she asked where Patrick Sullivan was. She saw the nurse's face. She knew. She knew the signs. She was catapulted back to her dad telling her that Ted was dead. Patrick was dead too. Their car had been hit by a drunk driver on their way from her house out onto I95.

Martha and the children had suffered some minor injuries but Patrick had taken the brunt of the collision. Maud was hysterical. She blamed herself for the accident. Only for her, Patrick would not have come in contact with that drunk. They would have gone home a different route and the children would be home safely tucked up in their beds, not in hospital beds waiting to be told that their dad was dead.

~~»»⟩ ⟨«««~

Maud stopped celebrating Christmas altogether after that. She went to a therapist. She understood the meaning of the word *accident* but she still felt that she fully deserved to carry around the blame for Patrick's death. Staying in Boston without Patrick was out of the question and staying on as company director wasn't possible either. She couldn't go into their office every day and look at his empty chair. She had gone there once since his death and her eyes had conjured him up. He was there talking to her, laughing, tossing balled-up paper into the trash, shouting *"Slam dunk!"* and jumping up and down like a kid. She knew she was on her way to having some kind of breakdown and couldn't risk going back to work. She had nothing left to give to the company. She had to get herself out of it for all of their sakes.

She worked out a deal with Warren and the cooperative and they bought her out and took over the operation immediately. She put blood money into a trust fund for Martha and the kids but this did nothing to assuage her guilt. Martha was kind and didn't blame her but Maud couldn't bear her kindness. She had to run away again.

# Chapter Eleven

"Dad, can I have the keys to the cottage in Inchahowen?"

"What? Why would you want to go there? There's no heating in it. I'm sure the roof is leaking too. Nobody's been there for years. Why don't you just stay put for a while? We'll figure it all out."

Maud couldn't stay put. She had been having dreams about the little cottage in West Cork where her grandfather had been born. It was left to her father but they hadn't been there for years. Her dad used to take them there when they were small. Her mom used to fly directly to Mémère in Paris and they would all join her there weeks later, having spent long summer days fishing for crabs, waiting for their dad while he had a pint in the local pub and running wild along the beaches and through the countryside.

Maud knew she had to go. She remembered how much Patrick had loved it there and always talked about fixing up the cottage and bringing his own children to West Cork to experience the carefree holidays they all had. Patrick wasn't going to be able to make it a reality but maybe she could.

Maud wasted no time. Her mind was made up and she booked flights and a rental car that evening. She could feel her parents' anxiety and she wished again that she was not the one giving the anxiety to them. They tried to talk her out of going but Maud's mind was made up.

Maud arrived in Inchahowen on a wild and windy day. The drive from Shannon airport did make her question her motivation once or twice as the car was almost blown off the road with the force of the gale that was blowing. The closer she got to the house, however, the calmer she felt and a sense of peace took the place of the nervousness. She pulled up outside the house which was in complete darkness and used the light of her phone to find the front door.

The cottage had a view of the wild Atlantic and a big nothing beyond but now there was nothing visible outside the window of the front room. Her dad was right, the place was freezing. She had stopped at a supermarket en route and picked up items she would need, having made a list on the plane. She lit a fire in the enormous fireplace. It took a while to catch and it just about took away the chill. The cold and damp was in the walls and no amount of fires would fix it, she reckoned as she ran her hands across the cold plaster.

Having made herself a cup of tea and eaten half a sandwich, she felt thoroughly exhausted. She climbed the narrow stairwell to the upstairs where she had the choice of two bedrooms. She took the one that she knew faced the sea and put on new bed linen that she had brought with her. The bed felt damp even with the new sheets. She lay in bed and worried she had bitten off more than she could chew.

She lay awake wondering what the hell she was doing there and why she didn't listen to her dad's sound advice. No point bitching about it now, she thought, and started to plan improvements to the cottage in her head. She would, of course, have to run the changes by her dad before she implemented any of them. And the local planning authority, she thought. But this was good. She was thinking about something other than Patrick and Ted. Two wonderful men she loved so much. She knew she needed something to take her mind off them or she would go crazy. A renovation project would be a good start.

She managed to sleep despite the cold and was surprised to see that it was eight thirty when she looked at her phone. She wasn't the slight bit disorientated and knew immediately upon waking where she was. For some reason she felt that for the first time in a long time she was where she was supposed to be.

She got out of bed and opened the curtains. The view almost took her breath away. She hadn't appreciated it as a kid. None of them did. The wild Atlantic roared and rolled only yards from where she stood. She felt like it was a part of her being and she welcomed the strength just looking at it gave her. No matter what the state the cottage was in, she thought, the location was perfect.

⇒⇒⇒ ⇐⇐⇐

The first thing she did every morning when she woke was to look out her window at the ocean. She decided she'd never again live away from the water. It had an energy and she was feeding off it. She could match her mood to it. Some days it was calm. Others stormy. It could change in a matter of minutes. The colours green and turquoise filled her head.

She wanted the cottage to reflect the ocean and she went into town to find the exact colours she was looking for. The nearest town was ten miles away and it seemed that everybody knew who she was, despite the fact that she had barely left the house, only to buy bread and milk in the village shop.

"You're the Sullivan girl, aren't ya?" they would ask. "Ah sure, I remember ye well – you and the little fellas running around in your bare feet and your poor father trying to keep up with ye. Ye were a wild bunch."

Maud liked that she had a connection to this place. She was glad that people respected her privacy. She didn't want to have to tell them that Patrick was dead. That the wild bunch had lost one of their number.

James gave Maud the go-ahead to make any changes she wanted to. He was happy that she had something to occupy her mind instead of blaming herself for Patrick. She drew up plans and hired a local builder to make her idea a reality. The planning process took a while but Maud had plenty to do in the meantime.

She knew the plans would be approved so she started shopping for the materials and furniture she would need. She mulled over different types of marble tiles which in fact didn't look very different from one another, worktops, beds and bathrooms until she thought her head would spin. She was responsible for each decision right down to which screws to use. By the time the project was finished and the cottage was an exact replica of her vision, she was too exhausted to enjoy it.

Then the days started to get longer and she started to get bored. She wasn't ready to go back to Boston but the loneliness was beginning to get to her. She knew it was her own fault that she was lonely. She had imposed the loneliness on herself by not accepting kind invitations from the locals to various events.

She needed to find something to do. She thought about setting herself up as an interior decorator but then decided she couldn't stomach it. She started to bake some cakes to keep her mind occupied. Then she couldn't stop. She made cupcakes and fruit cakes. She made croissants and pastries of all sorts. She baked from morning until night, trying to find comfort or meaning like she found in Paris. She gave it all away. To the postman, the hairdresser, her neighbours and anyone who would take them. She never wanted to eat any of it herself but it was good therapy for her.

Once again food was the thing that helped her heal. While she was out walking one day, she saw that the old fishing tackle shop was up for rent. She was wise enough to know that she needed to do something about her baking addiction. She also knew that she needed to look after her mental health. She needed to be among people again. She had even begun talking to herself in the little cottage. She would berate herself for little things and before she knew it, if she didn't take hold of herself, she would start answering herself back. The deal to lease the shop was sorted in half an hour. An old English gent who owned the shop was desperate to retire and thought he would be years waiting for a tenant to come along. When Maud approached him with her offer, he grabbed it with both hands.

# Chapter Twelve

Kate was the youngest of three girls and was the first person in her family to graduate from college. To be more accurate, she was the first one to finish school. Her sisters Emer and Grace left school early. Emer got pregnant at seventeen and had only ever held down a few part-time jobs since Kylie was born. Kate felt like an alien in her own home as working hard was all she ever wanted to do. She knew for sure it was the only way to get out of Inchahowen and out of her childhood home in particular.

It was a wonder that she managed to get herself through school at all. Her mother died when she was eight and, even at her young age, Kate felt that her mother was better off. She'd had a terrible life, thanks to Kate's dad. He had bullied and terrorised the whole lot of them for as far back as she could remember. He had worked when he got married first but soon decided that his time and money would be better spent in the pub. He drank every spare penny they had and occasionally drank the money that was meant for their food. The Harringtons were the local charity case. The community was small and everyone knew what everyone else had and didn't have. Kate never had new clothes or nice things. She figured out from an early age that anything she wanted she would have to get for herself. When their mother died, her two sisters, then twelve and thirteen, were skipping school and quit as soon as they were legally allowed. What was the point anyway, they concluded. They were both now as useless as their father. Thanks to her own determination and her teachers, Kate was saved from going down the same path. She was encouraged all the way through school by a handful of kind men and women who saw her potential and knew the difficulties facing her at home.

At school she found it easy to apply herself to her lessons but at home it was a completely different story. Emer's baby daughter was always squealing her head off and her father was still falling in the door stotious from drink. It was a chaotic scene day after day after day. Kate thought she would scream her own head off if she didn't get some quiet time to study.

"What has you giving out? You only have yourself to worry about. How would you like it if you had a baby to mind all day and all night?" Emer asked her after Kate complained that the noise of the baby crying was disrupting her study.

"If you had kept your legs crossed and your knickers on, you wouldn't have a baby to mind in the first place!" Kate retorted angrily.

"You are a stuck-up bitch, you know that? I'll get me own house now that I have a baby. When will you get your own place, smarthole?" Emer said, storming out of her room.

"I'll get everything I want. *Because I will bloody work my arse off for it!*" Kate shouted after her in total frustration.

Kate got a scholarship to study Business in college. She had applied through the school, knowing she would have no way to pay the fees herself. Once she got to Dublin, she got a part-time job and settled into college life. The freedom was something she had never imagined. Had never dared to imagine. She shared an apartment with two other girls. There were no screaming babies, no smelly nappies, no dirty dishes left in the sink for days. Although there were no rules written up anywhere, they respected each other's space and belongings and, for the first time ever, Kate truly believed her life was changing for the better.

Kate still went home every weekend and all but ran out of the house every Sunday night. Her father's drinking was getting worse and he spent most of his waking hours drunk. He used to be relatively sober for a couple of hours each day but now that time was less and less. He was a bad colour too and Kate suspected that his liver was damaged. She urged him to go to the doctor but of course he didn't go, saying that he'd prefer to spend the fifty euro in the pub and not give it to some quack doctor!

Her sisters were useless and so caught up in problems of their own making that they couldn't have cared less if their father was dead or alive. They had both moved to the town where they were renting houses practically next door to one another. Kate cursed the fact that she was the only one who was afflicted with a sense of duty to their father. She couldn't let him drink himself to death without making any effort to help him.

When a job came up in a telecoms company in Dublin, she wrestled with her conscience but decided to take it. She ordered her sisters to travel the ten miles every day on a rota to check on their father and, even though they bitched and moaned about it, they did it.

Kate loved the job and she loved Dublin. She was part of a big organisation and had got tons of experience and had lots of opportunity to climb the corporate ladder. She moved up very quickly and her earnings doubled in the first year. She was issued shares as part of her annual bonus which were worth a fortune. She never knew a feeling like it and was beginning to get a huge buzz out of having all this money to spend.

At the back of her mind she was feeling uneasy though. She imagined if her mother had had even a fraction of what Kate had in her bank account she could have fed her family for a year. Kate could only ever remember her mother struggling. She never had a car and Kate had images of her mother carrying the plastic shopping bags from the little shop in the village. Even if she had a car, she couldn't have gone to the supermarket in the bigger towns because she never would have had the money to spend there.

Kate remembered being sent to the village shop and the butcher to give them money to pay off their bill. Her mother got most of the food on credit and when, very occasionally, she was able to scrounge an extra few pounds from her husband, she paid off what she owed. *Jesus Christ.* It was so far removed from where Kate found herself now.

She wished her mother was still alive so she could treat her to some new clothes or nice meals. A holiday even. Her poor mother had a terrible life. Even though Kate blamed her father for that, she still felt responsible for him and when the call came that he was dying she knew she had to go home to Inchahowen. At the same time, the company was being taken over by an international telecoms giant and the staff were offered very generous redundancy packages. It seemed like it was meant to be and Kate packed up her small apartment and moved home again.

The house was filthy even though it was only her father there. Emer and Grace had kept up their end of the bargain and visited every day but they certainly didn't kill themselves cleaning the place. Once Kate came home, they were happy to hand over all duties to her and she hadn't seen sight nor light of either of them after she got back.

Her father was in the bedroom permanently and Kate was just trying to make him as comfortable as possible. A nurse came in every day in the morning and in the evening to check on him and administer his medication.

Kate held water to his lips and tried to spoon-feed him food that resembled what her sister would give to the baby. He fought against her constantly. He would not take a drink and would spit back the food at her. She wanted to give him a slap or shout at him but she had to exercise patience and be respectful of the fact that he was living out the final part of his life

Their dad had been a handsome man once. There was a wedding picture hanging upstairs under the Pope's blessing of their marriage. It always struck her, when she charged up or down the stairs as a child, that her parents looked happy in the picture. Kate had always assumed that it was because of them, the children, that they became the unhappy, miserable creatures they turned into.

It was only recently that it dawned on Kate that it was nothing to do with her or her sisters. Her uncles all left to go to America but her dad was deemed to be too young to go. He stayed behind with his widowed mother, Kate's grandmother, and looked after her. Stories had it that she wailed every day after her boys who had gone and treated Kate's dad like a skivvy. She was a bad, lazy woman who couldn't have cared less about her youngest child. She wouldn't let him go to school in case she would have to do any chore herself and as a result her father was almost illiterate and had no confidence. He did develop a charm which he learned to have around his mother, to coax her out of her fierce moods. When he met Maura, Kate's mother, he saw it as a way out of his mother's clutches. Maura fell for his good looks and charisma and they started going out. A few months later, Maura discovered she was pregnant. There was no question but they had to get married and pretend that the child was premature to avoid the scandal of having sex before marriage. Joe and Maura secured a council house, settled into married life and from what Kate could make out lived unhappily ever after.

Now here she was in the house they moved into after getting married, feeding her father from a spoon like he was a little baby. The indignity that old age brought on people was terrible and Kate felt that no matter how bad a husband and father he was, he deserved his family's help at the end of his days.

When Joe finally succumbed to death, Kate was glad that his suffering was over. She was happy that she had been there to ease his way from this life to the next one. She might not have liked him very much but she felt privileged to have been able to offer another human being some dignity and respect at the end of his life.

In the days and weeks that followed, Kate found herself wondering what it was all about. Was life something to be endured or enjoyed? Her thoughts swung between regret at leaving her job and relief at being free of all the bureaucratic bullshit and the corporate nonsense she used to have to deal with. No, she wouldn't run back cap in hand to her old employer. Nor would she jump straight back into the corporate world. She decided she'd take her time. She had a roof over her head and some money in the bank and she convinced herself that she would make the right move at the right time.

She saw the sign in the old fishing tackle shop when she was out walking one day. **Cake by the Ocean**. A new coffee shop promising the best bakes for miles. She then saw the other notice. **Staff wanted.** She took down the mobile number and later that night called Maud and secured a job in Inchahowen's newest business venture.

# Chapter Thirteen

Maud threw herself on the couch and kicked off her shoes. She was exhausted. She ached after a busy day on her feet and her hands were sore from piping the intricate decoration on each cake. She looked out her big window to the ocean beyond and she felt herself relax as the exhaustion left her muscles one by one.

She loved the old cottage. It was the perfect meld of old and new and the fact that it had been in her family for more than a century gave her a sense of belonging. It was also the perfect place to think. And Kate had given her food for thought. She didn't want Kate to leave but she knew the day would come. Inchahowen was too small to hold someone like Kate. She was beautiful and talented and needed the energy of a big city.

Kate had given Maud fair warning. She told her she wanted to own her own business, that she wanted to go into business with Maud, but only if they left Inchahowen. That was a deal-breaker for Maud. Kate didn't yet understand that Maud had done all that. Now she just wanted to power down.

The doorbell rang and disturbed Maud's thoughts. It was probably her neighbour, Danny. He sometimes called to see how she was doing.

She knew what he really wanted was to see if there was any surplus cake to be had. Maud always had something tasty for him. Including a glass of Jameson. She was so sure it was Danny that she didn't even check herself in the mirror.

Maud opened the door and beheld the most gorgeous man she had ever seen, standing there on her doorstep. His lips were moving and for some reason unknown to her, he looked displeased. It took her a few seconds to pull herself together and try to figure out what he was saying.

". . . and I don't think that it would do you any harm to let the old man walk his cows over your land. There's never been an issue for as long as my father and his father before him have farmed here."

He seemed to be more than a little bit angry with her but she had no idea why.

"*Em*, sorry. Who are you? What are you talking about?" She was genuinely bewildered now.

"I'm Tom Kennedy, Danny's son. He told me you were stopping him walking his cows over your land. It really is a terrible inconvenience for him. He's not getting any younger and if he has to make another path –"

"Hold on a minute! Danny told you that I was stopping him bringing his cows through? I have no idea why he'd say that." Maud's garden was bigger than she could handle or ever want. Her father had planted a row of hedging years before, making it more manageable. She had no interest in what went on beyond the hedge. Danny could be moving herds of elephants and she wouldn't give a damn.

"So you're saying he's lying?"

Maud was completely taken aback by Danny's son's bad attitude. "What I'm saying is that I have never even discussed his cows with your father. And you can tell him that he is *not* walking his cattle over my land until he damn well apologises to me. *Good night.*"

And with that she slammed the door in the handsome stranger's face. How bizarre was that? She turned to walk back to the comfort of her couch when she caught her reflection in the hall mirror. Oh my God, she looked like a banshee. Her hair was half up in a clip and the other half was sticking out in every possible direction. It looked dirty and greasy and her face didn't look much better.

She didn't normally look so dishevelled but it had been an extremely busy day. Oh God, there was a daub of dried cake batter stuck to her chin too. She could only imagine what that guy thought. What did he say his name was? Tom? He must have thought she was a complete lunatic.

She would call to Danny in the morning and find out what the hell he was playing at. She had been delighted to meet Danny when she moved in. It was nice to have a neighbour who hoovered up all the pastries she made and she was glad to chat to him, knowing that he was old and lived alone. In return for her kindness with her bakes, Danny did odd jobs around the garden for her. He would replace stones in the old stone wall and trim hedges that were getting out of hand.

She couldn't imagine what had gotten into Danny. She knew for sure she had never told him any such thing about moving his cows. Neither Danny nor his beloved cows ever bothered her. She hoped he wasn't developing some kind of dementia. He was probably in his late seventies, she thought. She decided she would visit him to assure herself that he was still fully compos mentis.

***

The next morning Maud was up early and took a little extra care getting herself ready. She wanted to make sure that she looked like a normal person, not someone who was AWOL from a lunatic asylum with dried food on her face.

She marched up to Danny's door, ready to have it out with the old guy or, more importantly, his son. She went to the back door and shouted Danny's name into the kitchen. She kinda hoped that Tom would be there. She wanted to see if he was really that handsome or if she had imagined it. But there was no sign of anybody.

The kitchen was messy so she went in and started to tidy away some breakfast things which were left on the table. So much for security! Danny was out and the house was wide open. OK, there didn't look like there was much worth taking but she would have to tell him to lock his door when he was out.

His son should have told him that. If he was any good, he would look out for his father, teach him to be more security-conscious and not call to her door accusing her of the nonsense he was talking about last night! She hoped he would appear so she could give him a piece of her mind. She continued to clean up until the kitchen was as tidy as her own.

When Maud got to work, the coffee shop was already open for business. The smell of sweet cakes baking brought a smile to her face as it always did. Kate was busy and mouthed a "hi" to her boss. Maud dropped her bag out back, put on her apron and was ready for action. The usual suspects were there and Maud could see how a girl like Kate would long for something less predictable and more exciting than this little cake shop in Inchahowen.

"I have something I need to talk to you about later on," she said to Kate as they passed each other with steaming cups of coffee.

"OK. I'm not in trouble, I hope," Kate said nervously.

"No, it's just something I was thinking about last night. I have a proposal for you."

Kate couldn't keep her mind on her work all during the breakfast rush. She needed to know if Maud was eventually going to do as she had urged and was going to expand the business. Maybe a joint venture. She had visions of them in the middle of Cork city in a fancy premises and being talked about in the papers.

By the time they eventually sat down to talk, in Kate's imagination she and Maud had opened stores in every major European City and just stopped short of New York City.

"I know it makes sense for you to move on and to get out of Inchahowen. I've been there and done that and have the T-shirt. I love the T-shirt, don't get me wrong, and I still wear it but I just don't want another one. But that's not to say that you shouldn't have a T-shirt of your own. In fact, I think you need one and that is why I am going to offer you the money to set up in business yourself. I will give you the money, be there to guide you in any way I can, but the rest is up to you. I won't be involved in a hands-on capacity."

"Hold on a minute! What are you saying? I was a bit thrown by all the T-shirt analogies. Are you saying what I think you're saying? Oh, Maud! *Oh my God!*"

She clapped her hands in delight and hugged Maud until she had to push her away, afraid she would crush her ribs.

"It is a business proposal, Kate," she said seriously. "We've got to keep it that way. If I don't see the merit in it, then I won't be investing. It's not personal. We've got to remember that."

"I understand. Thank you. Thanks for the opportunity. I will put my best proposal to you. I wouldn't insult you with anything less than my best."

Kate was buzzing for the rest of the day and Maud hoped that she would come up with a solid plan. She liked the idea of helping Kate get started but she was also not a woman who threw her money around lightly. The money she started out with was from Ted and there was no way she was going to fritter that away on anything that wasn't deserving.

When Maud was walking home that evening she saw Danny on the road, Ned his four-legged canine companion at his heels as usual.

"*Danny! Wait!*" she shouted after him.

He looked a bit sheepish and her anger at him abated slightly as she saw his lovely old wizened face.

"Hello, girleen. How are you today? Don't you look lovely altogether?" he said, in an attempt to get back into her good graces.

"You can knock that off. What are you doing telling your son I won't let you take the cows over my land? You know I don't have a problem at all with it. I can't even see what goes on behind that hedge. You know that. I really don't understand why you would say that. I thought we were friends."

"*Arah*, sure, I thought the two of you might hit it off. There was no way he was going to go over to your house and introduce himself to you. The two of you bein' single and all and sure I thought that maybe, well, you don't have a man, and sure he's on his own as well ... I thought that you two would ... you know ... *er* ... Well, I just thought you might like each other if you ever met."

"What? *Jesus*, Danny! You're a real piece of work! I used to like you, you know. But you can forget about me baking you any more cakes. Or inviting you in for a drop of whiskey. That was a rotten thing for you to do, Danny Kennedy. I don't know if I will ever forgive you."

"He's a fine-lookin' fella though, isn't he, girleen?" Danny said with a glint in his eye.

"You are a bad man, Danny. I'm going now and I haven't decided if I want to talk to you again."

But Maud was smiling as she walked away. She had to admire Danny's efforts. And he was right. His son was a fine-looking fellow indeed.

# Chapter Fourteen

Kate was eventually satisfied with her business plan. She checked and rechecked it. She hoped Maud would be impressed. She envisioned a city-centre premises with a big kitchen and just a smattering of seating and tables. She decided she had to be in Dublin. Cork was too small for her ambitions. She had contacted estate agents who had given her lists of vacant properties in the city centre. Because of the tech companies policies on working from home, there were more commercial premises available and at better rates than in previous years. She averaged out rents and council rates and felt she had covered all bases.

She arranged to call to Maud's house one evening after work to present it to her and she handed it over like it was the most precious thing in the world. All she could do now was wait to hear what Maud thought of it.

She had been doing her research for quite a while even before Maud had made her proposition. She knew there was a huge market for creations and confections like they had in Inchahowen. Even in a small seaside village, people were clamouring for Maud's over-the-top creations. They were so beautiful to look at in the first place and they were also something of a status symbol. Homemade cakes were embarrassing at birthday parties these days.

But it wasn't only birthdays and private events that Kate had in mind. She had the corporate market in her sights and she would tap every contact she ever had for business. Nobody was doing it and she was brimming over with new ideas. Companies were merging, rebranding, scaling up and starting up all the time and Kate knew that each event could be marked with an enormous innovative impressive over-the-top cake that she created. She was excited and confident and couldn't wait for Maud to read her plan.

⤜⤜⤜  ⤛⤛⤛

In fairness to Kate, Maud wanted to give her an answer as soon as she could. She went over the business plan and wished she had Patrick's insight and business brain. But even without Patrick's expertise, she could see that Kate's ideas and her figures stacked up. Kate would open the first dedicated OTT Cake Shop in the capital city. It was a copy and paste of what they were doing at Cake by the Ocean, but on a much grander scale.

There were of course tons of existing bakeries in the city but none were as outrageous and extraordinary as the one Kate had in mind. She had a vision of her cakes being at every brand launch for every business in the city. Kate was just as good with people as she was with cake batter and fondant. Her secret weapons were her sharp mind and bright bubbly personality. She would be her own best salesperson.

Maud didn't think for a minute that setting up the business would be an easy task for Kate but she knew that Kate had as good a chance if not better than most of pulling it off.

It took Kate days to settle down after getting the news from Maud that all systems were go for OTT Cakes. Then both women went to Dublin to look at properties and agreed on a premises near the docklands immediately. The location was amazing and was close to the Dart station. The shop itself seemed to be full of character and original fixtures and fittings. Kate and Maud looked at each other and pinched each other's hands. They didn't want to give it away to the estate agent as they knew the rent would shoot up if he knew how badly they wanted it. They made him bring them to several other locations just to disguise their enthusiasm. Once they had seen all locations, they told the estate agent that they would need to think it over and that they were going to see more properties the following day with another agent.

Happily, they secured the premises. Kate could see her old office from where she stood outside the shop and was excited beyond words. Maud drove them both back to Inchahowen and Kate dozed in the passenger seat and dreamed of her new cake shop decorated in pink, black and white.

The women got down to the nitty-gritty of the signing of contracts. It was agreed that Kate would repay Maud over a period of three years but that Maud would retain a twenty-percent stake in the business with an option for Kate to buy her out after five years. Maud insisted that Kate get proper advice before she signed up to anything and when both women were satisfied with the arrangements in place, they both signed the documents for the setting up of OTT Cakes.

# Chapter Fifteen

At four o'clock on Christmas Eve, Maud waved goodbye to her last cake of the Christmas season. Honestly, the orders were crazy this year. She turned the sign on the door to '*Closed*', slowly and deliberately twisted the key and locked the door. She let out a sigh of relief tinged with some sadness. When she reopened after the holiday season, Kate wouldn't be there.

She would miss Kate both as an employee and as a friend and find her hard to replace. Maud imagined this was what parents felt like when their kids went off to college, scared for them but resigned to the fact that they couldn't stay at home forever.

She turned around to see Kate putting on her coat, getting ready to leave.

"Well, that was nuts," Kate said, pulling her hat over her glossy curls.

"Yeah, mental note to myself not to have cake orders still to fill on Christmas Eve."

"I'll believe that when I see it," Kate said. "Sure I'll be the same when I open OTT. When I'm working for myself, I'll find it hard to turn down business."

"Is this really the last day we'll work together? I'm gonna miss you."

"I'm going to miss you too. We worked hard but we had some great laughs too. And what you're doing for me, Maud – I'm so grateful."

"It's a new exciting chapter for you. And I know you're going to smash it."

Kate hoped that she lived up to Maud's hype. But she didn't have time to think about it now. She had to go home and get glammed up to go out and meet her pals in Seán's pub in the village. Lots of her friends were home for Christmas and she couldn't wait to see them all.

"You're still planning on coming to Seán's later?" she said. "It'll be great craic. There's always a great atmosphere there on Christmas Eve."

Seán's was the only pub in Inchahowen. The sign over the door said *The Do Come Inn* but the locals joked that Sean was so cranky it should read *The Don't Bother Your Arse Coming Inn*.

"What else am I gonna do?" said Maud. "Sit at home and wait for Santa Claus?"

"Great. I'm glad you're coming. I've told my friends all about you and they're dying to meet you."

"I can't imagine why."

"Because you're beautiful and funny and incredibly talented. That's why. And you better turn up, lady. No excuses like falling asleep on the couch will be accepted."

"I'll be there. I think we deserve a few glasses of champagne after such a busy day, don't you?"

"Champagne. You'll be lucky. I'd say you'll be doing well to get a bottle of cheap Prosecco in Seán's!" Kate laughed. Seán's was very much a local pub with the emphasis on pints of porter, not fancy wines and champagne.

"Once it's cold and sparkly, I won't mind," Maud said, giving Kate a hug.

"We live in hope," said Kate, returning the hug and thanking Maud for the millionth time for believing in her.

"Just prove me right. See you later on."

⤞⤝

Maud let herself into her house. The underfloor heating ensured the house was always toasty warm. She made straight for the kitchen and poured herself a glass of champagne which she had left chilling in the fridge. She put on some music and raised a silent toast to her family and to those who were gone.

Maud had loved Christmas when she was younger, but fate had determined that she wasn't going to enjoy it as an adult. She remembered, as a child at home in Boston it would snow almost every Christmas. She and her brothers couldn't wait for their dad to finish his shift at the hospital and get home to his brood.

She didn't know if she imagined it or not but she had an image of her and her brothers leaning on the back of the couch looking out the window waiting for the first sign of him coming up the steps. There was always a huge tree in the living room and the five red wool stockings hung in expectation from the huge mantelpiece over the fireplace. Christmas carols filled the air.

Hélène loved Christmas too and each year made it her mission that everything would be perfect. And it always was. Well, it always was in Maud's memories. If her dad was working on Christmas Day and couldn't make it home, then Hélène would announce that they were moving Christmas Day until the following day.

But Santa always came on Christmas Eve, no matter what her dad's roster was. Sure there were fights or some of the boys would be in trouble for something or other but these never surfaced in her mind when she thought of her childhood Christmases.

Maud would Facetime her parents on Christmas morning. They were spending Christmas in Paris with Marielle who had been suffering from bad health for the past few years and Hélène was afraid that it might be her last Christmas. They had asked Maud to go to Paris with them but her hectic schedule wouldn't allow it. Her brothers were all getting together for Christmas Day and Maud was looking forward to seeing her gorgeous nieces and nephews. She hoped they liked the gifts she had sent them. She was always very generous and she had the status of favourite aunt among them all.

Hélène and James were making a stop in Inchahowen before flying back to Boston. Of course, they would wear their usual baffled faces as they pondered why she chose to live on her own in a remote village on the Atlantic Ocean and not with the family who loved her and missed her. Nonetheless the thought of seeing her parents filled her with joy.

Maud had a couple of hours to spare before she met Kate, so she ran a bath. She lit some candles and relaxed in the warm bubbles, sipping her glass of Moet. She was lying back in the sudsy water and felt the tiredness leaving her. She tried to think happy thoughts but it didn't take long for the lonely feelings to catch up on her.

The loneliness crept in at her quietest moments. *Come on!* She was trying here. Like really trying. Hell, she had even put up twinkly lights and Christmas music was playing on the music system. But her brain had to keep reminding her that she was all alone at Christmas. OK, she'd have her family on video, but that was no substitute for the real thing.

She had no one person to shower her love and affection on. She had no one true love. And weren't they fed this narrative over and over? You were nobody until somebody loved you. The saddest thought was that Ted had been the love of her life and that she might never experience that kind of love ever again.

But surely she wouldn't have this longing for love if there was never going to be anybody who would satisfy it? That would be cruel. She hoped that just like her beautiful house lay waiting for her, some guy was out there waiting for her to claim him.

She felt bad for thinking of the things she lacked in her life instead of being thankful for the wonderful things that she did have. She chastised herself and shrugged off the lonely thoughts. She stepped out of the bath and dried herself off with a fluffy towel.

She wrapped her hair in a towel and flipped through the clothes in her wardrobe, wondering what to wear. From talking to Kate earlier, it sounded like her friends got really dressed up when they went out, even if it was only to the local pub. She hadn't dressed up in ages. She couldn't remember the last time she wore clothes that weren't jeans, sweatpants or shorts. She looked like a boy most of the time. She wondered if it was some kind of attempt to hide from the world. *Fuck,* she thought, I need to make an effort.

She looked at the dresses which were in another section of her wardrobe. She had a lot of them. A reminder of her life in Boston. She picked out a sapphire-blue dress that sparkled like a jewel and picked up the blue of her eyes. She put it on and then found some matching stiletto heels. She remembered wearing the outfit to the opening of an art exhibition in the gallery in Beacon Hill. Ted was with her. It seemed like another lifetime.

She got a bit of a surprise when she looked in the mirror. She had forgotten what she used to look like. She was so used to wearing an apron to work that she hadn't seen her figure in a long time.

She used the hot wand on her hair and blonde curls fell over her shoulders. She added some make-up and sprayed her wrists and neck with the Tom Ford perfume that Ted used to wear. The scent sent her back to their house in Back Bay. To Ted. But for some reason she didn't feel like bursting into tears. She felt like he was happy for her. Cheering her on from the sidelines.

She gave herself one last glance in the mirror. She might be mingling with girls who were ten years younger than her but she sure as hell wasn't going to look it.

# Chapter Sixteen

Seán's was packed to the rafters. Maud could hardly believe that this many people lived in Inchahowen. She looked and saw Kate waving frantically at her and gesturing for her to come over.

"The seats are like gold dust," she said, giving the free seat to Maud. "I'm so glad you're here – to be honest, I didn't think you'd come. You look absolutely fantastic by the way."

"Of course I came. I said I would, didn't I?" She smiled at her friend.

Kate made the introductions and, true to her word, Kate's friends were charming and friendly. Most were working abroad and were thrilled to be back to spend Christmas with their families. They seemed like very accomplished bunch and Maud imagined that most of them wouldn't ever move back home for good.

After a short time in their company, Maud felt like she was part of the gang. They were doing shots and drinking like it was going out of fashion. Maud found herself draining her glasses furiously too. She was on her fifth glass of champagne. The bartender had found a dusty bottle in the back of the storeroom. Luckily the storeroom was freezing and the champagne was therefore chilled.

On her way to and from the bar, Maud met a lot of women who were regulars at the cake shop. They were all agog at how well she scrubbed up! She tried not to be insulted by their shocked expressions. She knew that she never looked glamorous while working but she must really look like a ogre if the reaction of these women was anything to go by.

She knew the women but they weren't friends. She always stopped herself from getting too involved with anybody. She knew if she was friends with them she'd have to tell them all about Ted and Patrick. She couldn't bear their pity.

Maud ordered herself not to think any sad thoughts tonight and concentrated on having a good time. She was feeling a little drunk and excused herself to go to the bathroom. She really couldn't knock back another glass of champagne or she'd be on her ear.

On the way to the ladies' room she bumped into Danny. Literally. He looked very pleased to see her and almost squeezed the life out of her. This was not an altogether pleasant experience as she imagined it had been a long time since Danny had acquainted himself with a bar of soap. He was wearing smart clothes, obviously in honour of the Christmas season but they too must not have been cleaned for an age.

"You're a sight for sore eyes, so you are! Who woulda known you were that pretty? You don't look any great shakes with those overalls you wear in the shop." He stood back to admire her.

"Thanks, I think," said Maud, wondering if there was a compliment in there somewhere.

"Did I introduce you to my son?" he said, and with that Tom appeared at his side.

Danny knew full well that he had already instigated an introduction but he had chosen not to mention it. What a guy!

"I've had the pleasure, thanks," said Maud, extremely happy to see Tom again.

"Hi! Look, I'm really sorry about calling to your house that night. He told me what he did." He pointed at his father.

"I'll leave you two youngsters to get acquainted," said Danny.

Off he went, leaving Maud and Tom looking at each other, wondering how Danny had managed to do this again.

"He told me you were being a right ... Well, I won't repeat what he said. He wants me to think he can't cope here by himself and needs me around the place. He really is testing my patience. I had to fly back from London today because he told me he was having a heart attack and that he was going to ring the ambulance to take him to the hospital. I jumped on the first flight and then I get here and he's out counting the cattle, right as rain."

"Are you serious? *Gee*, you gotta give him credit for that stunt." Maud was genuinely amazed at the lengths Danny was going to, to get his son to come home, but she could tell that Tom was fuming and decided against more praise for Danny's ingenuity. "Sorry," she said, squeezing by him. "I'm just on may way to the bathroom. It was nice to meet you again."

What the hell am I doing, she thought? She should have stayed talking to him. Or just looking at him. He was divine. She glanced back.

He had now gone back to the bar to talk to his father. Damn, she really wanted to talk to him some more.

Back at her table a few minutes later, she could see him from the corner of her eye, sitting at the bar with Danny. She felt his eyes on her a few times and caught him stealing glances at her too. He didn't look away like she expected him to, but gave her what she could only describe after several glasses of champagne as smouldering looks.

Suddenly it was closing time, which wasn't determined by licensing laws but by Seán himself depending on whether he felt like kicking them all out and going to bed or serving all night.

Kate and her friends were leaving to go to some nightclub in town. They begged Maud to go with them but she couldn't think of anything she wanted to do less than go to a sweaty nightclub and down several more drinks. There was only one reason she would get sweaty and that reason was standing ten feet away from her at the bar.

She was about to follow Kate and her friends outside, when Tom and Danny walked by and said goodnight to her.

"*Eh*, goodnight then. Merry Christmas," she managed to mutter to her neighbour and his devastatingly handsome son.

Kate and her friends were already out the front door. Tom gave one last glance at her standing there all alone and he too disappeared.

She could hardly contain her disappointment that he was gone. She felt like the air had been sucked out of the pub and had an overwhelming need to get out of there. The champagne high was threatening to leave her too. She felt the onset of a hangover and already dreaded waking up the following morning.

And she was now going to be alone again. Great, she thought as she gathered up her belongings and said her "Merry Christmases" as she walked out through the packed pub.

As she set out to walk the couple of hundred yards to her house, she was imagining what Tom's mouth would feel like on hers. She imagined him kissing her gently at first and then with more gusto. Her dreamy thoughts were interrupted then.

She looked up and Tom was by her side.

"I came back to walk you home. I should have thought to ask you when we were leaving if you wanted to come with us – please excuse my bad manners."

"It's fine. I'm capable of getting myself home," she said, suddenly tripping and nearly falling into a pothole on the road.

Tom caught her by the arm and held her until he was sure she had regained her balance.

*Shit!* Well, she'd thought she was capable of getting herself home without disappearing into a hole never to be seen again. He was kind enough not to laugh and she was grateful for that.

"Damn shoes!" she said.

"They look lethal," he replied.

"Yeah, I'll stick to my sneakers in future."

"Probably wouldn't look great with the dress though."

"True," she giggled, amused that she was discussing fashion with Danny's handsome son.

They were mostly silent on the way home, the only sound the clip-clip of Maud's stiletto heels on the tarmac road. Once they got to Maud's driveway she was glad that Tom turned in as well. He was walking her to her door. She was enjoying being in such close proximity to this sexy man. She wished she had a longer driveway that went on for miles and he would have to walk her the whole way but, almost the moment she had the thought, they were already at her front door.

"When are you going back to London?" she asked.

"I'll spend Christmas Day with the old man. No choice in the matter at this stage – there are no flights on Christmas Day. I would prefer to be in London with Molly, my daughter, watching her opening her presents on Christmas morning but my father had other ideas. My wife, I mean my ex-wife, is going balistic that I'm missing it.."

"It's not like you did it on purpose. You came to see your sick dad. Even though he's not actually sick, but she must understand that."

Tom laughed. "Valerie would have to look up the meaning of '*understand*' in the dictionary. I have strict instructions to pick up Molly up at three o'clock sharp on Boxing Day. Valerie has a party she's going to. She's been talking about it since October, so God help me if I am the reason she misses it."

Maud was staring at Tom and wondering how anybody could be angry with him. She loved everything about him. His accent was a mix of West Cork and posh English. She could listen to him forever.

"Anyway, I want to spend all the time I can with Molly. She's the best thing that ever happened to me. I worry that she feels like some sort of commodity that's being passed around between us. Sorry. I don't know why I'm telling you all of this. I'm sure you're not interested in the details of my personal life."

*Au contraire, mon frère!* She was interested in every single, tiny, little minute detail of his personal life. "I'm happy to hear about your life. Would you like to come in? For a nightcap?" *A nightcap.* Jesus, who said that nowadays? She was definitely under the influence of alcohol.

"*Em.* Yes, sure, I'd like that."

"I have whiskey, is that OK?"

"Perfect."

She let him in the front door into the big kitchen-living-room which housed her massive sofa and in the daylight afforded her the amazing views of the Atlantic Ocean. He seemed to be really impressed with her home and commented on the mix of old and new like a man who knew what he was talking about.

"Sorry, it's a hazard of the job. I'm an architect. I have my own practice in London. I have designed my dream home in my head and on paper many times and it's not a million miles away from this. OK, it's not in Inchahowen but I'm staggered at how like it this is. Who designed it for you?"

"Nobody actually, I designed it myself," she said, taking pride in what she had achieved. "This is my dad's house but he gave me free rein to do as I pleased. He used to bring me and my brothers here when we were kids but nobody has used it in years. My mom and dad are getting older and coming to a place with no heating and a hole in the roof wasn't enticing. I lived in it for a while to see exactly what it was missing and what could make it better. I love the thick old walls but I also love the glass. I wake up every day to the sea."

They both took a moment to appreciate the space.

"What kind of buildings do you design?" she asked.

"Mainly industrial stuff now. I started out tendering to design social housing for a London borough and got the job. The practice got an award for it and then all of a sudden we were being asked to do similar schemes. I must say I'm very impressed with your design. If you're ever looking for a job, I'd be glad to hire you. When I see a house like this, it makes me nostalgic for the thrill of creating a space where someone can live. I don't mean just live day to day. I mean a place where you can live your best life. Where you can be your best self because your surroundings allow you to be. That probably sounds a bit fanciful." He looked slightly embarrassed.

"No, I know exactly what you mean. When I walked into this house, even though it was rundown and maybe shoulda been knocked down, I knew that I was going to be able to think clearly here and to make good decisions. Every nook and cranny spoke to me." She looked up at him. "Now I sound fanciful."

"How convenient if we both turned out to be."

He looked away but she was sure she'd seen something like a connection in his eyes.

"How about that nightcap?" he said.

"Oh yeah, sure, coming right up." She went to the kitchen cabinet and took out two tumblers. She poured two fingers of whiskey in each one.

"Ice?"

"Please. Two."

While she was in the kitchen she put on a Spotify Christmas album and connected it to her speaker.

They sat on the couch and watched the twinkly lights, sipping their drinks. Bing Crosby was crooning about a white Christmas through the speaker system and Maud started to think it might be a very merry Christmas after all.

"So, your dad is some guy, huh?" she said eventually. "He must want you to come back here real bad. Faking a heart attack and all. Do you think you would come back here some day?" She was praying that he didn't catch the hopefulness in her question.

"No. My life is in London now. I am too tied to the place in every sense. My practice is there, my daughter is there. I'm afraid old Danny will have to resign himself to that fact and the sooner the better. I told him that I won't just hop on a plane the next time he calls me."

"What if it really is an emergency, though? How would you forgive yourself if you didn't come?"

"Mrs. Pierce up the road normally keeps an eye on him. And I know you do too. Thank you for that. The reason he tried it on this time is that Mrs. Pierce is away visiting her son for Christmas and he knew I couldn't ring her to check if he was telling the truth. He's an awful man. In the best sense of the word, of course! He will probably outlive me, considering the stress he's causing me. Speaking of which, I'd better go back to see if the old codger is alright."

He drank off the last of his whiskey and got up to leave.

"Thanks for the drink." He looked out over the black ocean out the huge window to the lighthouse on the headland beyond. "I would love to see the view from here in daylight. Although I'm sure I have already seen it in my head a thousand times."

"You're welcome to come and look at my view anytime." Did she just say that? What was wrong with her tonight? The champagne had done the damage so she thought it best to say very little from then on.

When she opened the door, they both stepped onto the porch and looked towards the lighthouse in the distance.

He turned back to look at her and bent his head to kiss her. Maud felt his soft lips on hers and felt her insides melting. She put her hands to his cheeks and felt his stubble there. The softness of his kiss was at odds with the prickly skin beneath her fingertips and she never wanted him to stop. The kiss got more intense but then he stopped kissing her and moved away. She felt herself sway and wondered if it was the effects of the alcohol or the kiss making her unsteady.

"Well, goodnight," she said. What the hell? Could she not for once come up with something sexy or witty to say?

"Goodnight, Maud Massachusetts. By the way you look really good without the cake mix on your face. Really beautiful, in fact." And with that he kissed her lightly on the lips and was gone over the fields to Danny's.

Maud Massachusetts? Is that what he called her? And he had noticed the dried cake mix on her face the last time they met. Crap. But, oh my God! What a kiss! What a kisser! She wanted to fall asleep and dream of that kiss and never wake up. But he would be gone tomorrow and he had said he might not be back for a while. But, like Scarlett

O'Hara, she wouldn't think about that now. After all, tomorrow was another day.

# Chapter Seventeen

Tomorrow certainly was another day but it wasn't a good one. Christmas Day brought a monumental hangover that Maud thought would never go away. She spent most of the morning lying on the cold tiles on her bathroom floor. That was only after finding the switch to turn off the underfloor heating and suffering in her warm bed until the tiles cooled down.

She longed to feel like a human being again. Even the thought of last night's beautiful kiss could not ease the nausea and headaches that came crashing down. She began to recount how many drinks she had and felt ill all over again. The answer was way too much.

It wasn't usual for her to drink and she would be getting back into that habit of not doing so straight away. She was grateful her parents were not arriving until the day after tomorrow. She might be feeling better by then.

Once the hangover abated, her thoughts went straight back to Tom and the kiss. She began to question if it had actually taken place or if it was the imaginings of a drunken lush. But she knew it had to be real. It was the best thing that had happened to her in a long time. She relived it over and over again and it was getting more wonderful as her hangover lifted.

It was after four in the afternoon when she finally left her room. She wrapped herself in her blanket and dragged it and herself to the kitchen. Darkness was beginning to fall and the Atlantic looked wild and green and angry. Green, a bit like she felt herself.

She had missed the daylight part of Christmas. Not that she cared too much. Christmas was just another day. This was the only way she managed not to blubber her way through it. She saw the open whiskey bottle and the two glasses on the kitchen counter. She screwed the lid back on and put the bottle at the back, way at the back of the kitchen cabinet.

She lifted up the glasses to put them in the dishwasher. She touched the glass without lipstick marks, the one he had touched with his lips. She put her fingers instinctively to her mouth and felt the warm pressure of his lips on hers all over again. God, she needed to get out more. If a man she had only ever met once before had this effect on her she was definitely lacking excitement in her life.

She tried to remember the conversation they'd had but all she could remember was the kiss. She couldn't stop putting her fingers to her lips and felt the beginnings of butterflies in the pit of her stomach. Like the hangover, the thought of the kiss would have disappeared by tomorrow and she could get back to being her normal self.

Hélène and James arrived in Inchahowen on December 27<sup>th</sup> to howling winds and torrential rain. Maud had made the cottage very cosy with a big fire lighting and candles lit all around. She hoped that the cosiness would distract her mom from the fact that she was living on her own, in a cottage in a remote village on the edge of the Atlantic, three thousand miles from home.

They spent two days walking along the beaches and coves nearby and talking. Not talking so much as Maud answering her mom's million questions. When things started to get hairy, James usually made himself scarce and left the women to it.

"Maud, I don't care what you say, it cannot be good for you to be here all alone."

Her mother's worried expression tugged at Maud's heartstrings. "Mom, I'm perfectly happy here. I have my shop, my friends and, most importantly, I have time to myself. You know I'm happier on my own." She was attempting to justify her choices.

"Nonsense. You never used to want to be on your own. You were the wildest girl I ever knew. Your father and I were over the moon when we got our little girl after all the boys. But you were just like one of them. If I tried to dress you in frills, I swear you got yourself dirty on purpose. I don't remember you alone when you were growing up. Ever. I don't even think I have a photograph of you on your own apart from the ones taken in grade school. You were always in the middle of everything. How can you have changed so much? Tell me, *ma petite*, because I cannot make any sense of it at all."

"It's no big deal, Mom. I'm connected to you all constantly. It's not like the old days when, if you lived in a different country, you never got to see each other. I'm on Facetime every other day with one of you. We're probably more in touch now than we would be if I was still in Boston. So don't think I'm alone."

"I think you have cut yourself off on the inside. It's not your fault. How many times do I have to tell you this? It's not your fault, my beautiful girl," Hélène pleaded with her.

"Mom, people I loved died. I can't just flip a switch and, hey presto, I'm over it. I am trying though. Honestly I am. And I'm getting there. I'm making progress but it's slow. Please don't keep worrying about me cos that makes me worry about you. It's like we've created a big vicious worry circle."

They eventually agreed to drop the subject, much to Maud's relief.

The days flew by and suddenly it was time for her parents to leave.

To Maud's great surprise, despite all the interrogation and feeling like she was a huge disappointment to them, she missed them as soon as they were gone.

# Chapter Eighteen

Tom sat behind his desk with his head in his hands. His hands were partially covering his ears and he could hear snippets of what Andrew, his accountant, was saying to him. Things like: lose some staff ... no bonus payments ... cut expenses ... There was nothing coming out of Andrew's mouth that he liked or, to be honest, that he didn't expect to hear.

"Can they do this? Stop the build just like that?" Tom asked.

"Seemingly it's in the contract," replied Andrew, who had been a friend and employee of Tom for over twenty years.

"Seemingly? For fuck's sake, Andy. Get Jeremy and the whole fucking legal team over here *now*."

Tom couldn't believe what he was hearing. Kennedy Architects had designed and were project-managing a multi-million-pound state-of-the-art plant for Gilbrade Pharmaceuticals in Belfast. Years of work had gone into tendering for the contract and, when they eventually won it, Tom had hired the best team of engineers and designers in the world. All at a hefty cost.

He fumed silently at his desk as Andrew made a call. A few moments later Jeremy, his in-house solicitor, was in the office.

"So? They can't do this, right?" Tom asked him.

"Yes and no."

"What do you mean? I presume we're protected. We'll be compensated? Jeremy, I've got hundreds of thousands of pounds in payroll every month, never mind the running costs of the business besides."

"They can delay the build for six months before any compensation kicks in," Jeremy replied.

"*Six months?* Kennedy Architects will be dead and buried long before then. How the hell did we allow them to put a condition like that into the contract? *Jesus fucking Christ!*"

"We argued it with their legal team but they insisted it was left in. We had this discussion, you and I. We figured, with Gilbrade turning over billions a year and the fact that the plant is being built for that new weight-loss drug, that it would never be an issue."

Well, it certainly was an issue now. Tom wanted to kick himself. He was sure that Jeremy had run it by him, he just didn't remember. There had been so many decisions to make. A team to hire. He was getting divorced. How could he have been so stupid?

"We've got to fight this."

"But the contract states …"

"I don't give a *fuck* what the contract states, Jeremy! I am not going to sit idly by and watch everything I worked for go down the drain. I am going to fight those fuckers!"

Tom knew a journalist who worked at *Business Weekly* and decided to give him a call. Simon York was well known for his investigative journalism and digging beneath a company's figures and balance sheets to find out how they came up with the bottom line.

Simon and Tom had been groomsmen for Andrew ten years earlier when he married Joanna. They had played a few pranks on the groom and had struck up a good friendship. Simon had done a few stories on Tom's successes over the years.

Tom dialled his mobile number.

"Tom, how are you?" said the very British voice.

"Good, Simon, good. Sorry to bother you but I need to talk to you off the record if that's OK."

"Of course, old chap. Fire away."

"I was wondering if you heard anything on the grapevine about Gilbrade Pharmaceuticals? They've just stalled the build on the facility in Belfast. We're in the middle of project-managing it. Mea culpa, I put all Kennedy's Architects' eggs into one basket. But I thought the basket was sturdy."

"That's the plant for the weight-loss drug? This is very much off the record but I did hear that the trials results aren't what they hoped. Some side affects they're worried about. I'll tell you what, I'll have a root around, make a few calls and get back to you. Give me a day or two. I'd like to have the full story, not some half-assed rumour and innuendo bit of stuff."

"Thanks, Simon. I'd appreciate anything you could find out. There are livelihoods at stake."

"That's what friends are for," said Simon. "By the way, how are you doing? I'm sure Christmas was a bit of a nightmare, first one being divorced etc." Simon coughed nervously, no doubt feeling he might have intruded on his friend's personal business.

"It was a nightmare in a lot of ways. My father decided he was having a heart attack on Christmas Eve. I had to hop on a flight. It would have been cheaper to fly to New York and back a few times but I had to do it. I got to Cork and had to rent a car which I could have bought for the amount they charged me. I'm not complaining about the cost but the old bastard was out herding cattle when I got there. Not a bother on him. With all the stress I was nearer to having the heart attack than he was." Tom recalled the 'planes, trains and automobiles' day he had.

"Jesus Christ! Sounds like he'll stop at nothing to get you back home!" said Simon, laughing at Danny's attempts to bring Tom home to Inchahowen.

"That's not the half of it. I called to his neighbour and berated her for no good reason at all – a lovely American woman who has the misfortune of living next door to him. He'd made up some story about her not allowing him to use her land to ... anyway, a city boy like you wouldn't understand the arrangement they have but, let's just say, he was actually trying to set us up. I'd swear he's hoping I'll fall in love with her and decide to move back. Jesus, he's worse than a child!"

"And what's she like?"

"Who?"

"The American. What's she like?"

"*Eh,* quite attractive. Actually she is very attractive. I haven't given it much thought but she is quite lovely. If I had the time or the inclination to date again, which I most definitely do not, she'd be pretty high on the list."

Tom then thought of the kiss on Christmas Eve. He hadn't had much time to think about it since it happened but now a warm feeling rose up in him when he remembered the feel of her lips and how soft her skin and hair were. How she smelled.

"Interesting. Look, old chap, I'll get onto it straight away and bell you tomorrow or the next."

They hung up and Tom felt a little calmer. He just hoped that Simon would find out something, anything, that could somehow save his company.

# Chapter Nineteen

It was late on New Year's Eve and Maud had settled in for the night. She thought about her parents, now safely back in Boston. She admired their resilience and assumed it came with age. They had known so much joy and loss in their lives but they seemed to be able to keep the show on the road and stay positive.

She was just about to go upstairs and put on her pyjamas when there were a few loud knocks on her door. Could it be him? No, he'd gone back to London. But maybe he'd come back for some reason. Her stomach flipped as she forced herself not to run to the door.

It was Danny. In the disappointment of seeing the old man standing there, Maud didn't know if she was supposed to be mad at him or not.

"Danny! I thought the riot police were here with all the banging," she said, deciding that she was very much still annoyed with him.

"Will you come and give me a hand, lass? I have a cow calving and she's in trouble. The vet, the useless fucker, is out at some fancy dinner and ball and won't be able to come until the morning. It'll be too late by then. She's in an awful state, so she is."

Danny seemed genuinely shaken. She'd kill him if this was another "cry wolf" story.

"Jeez, Danny, how can I help? I make cakes for a living. Oh hell, I suppose I can try!" She grabbed her wellington boots from the under the stairs and wrapped herself up against the cold.

"You're a good lassie, so you are," said Danny as he ran through the field towards his sheds.

Maud knew nothing about animals but, when she saw the cow lying in the straw, she knew she was in a lot of distress. Some kind of caring instinct took over and she went to the cow and started to rub her head. She had never noticed how lovely cows were before but, when she looked into her eyes, she saw something almost human there.

The sound the cow made was coming from somewhere Maud couldn't quite fathom. Her friends and sisters-in-law had shared videos of them having babies and Maud was amazed at the level of pain the women experienced. But the women were able to avail of an epidural when the pain became too hard to bear. This poor cow would have no such relief. Maud wanted to let the cow know that she was there rooting for her. She felt as useless as a man when his partner was experiencing all the pain and knowing there was nothing he could do only be there.

She kept rubbing the cow's head while Danny was lost somewhere at the cow's other end. Maud looked at one stage and saw that most of his arm was inside the cow, trying to bring on the calf. The cow was exhausted. She had been in labour for hours, Danny had said, and she was worn out. Maud now too cursed the useless fucker of a vet who put a New Year's Eve ball ahead of a poor animal's welfare.

"It might have been the cord," Danny said. "I've freed it now, I think. Let's give her a minute and see if the urge to push kicks in."

Maud was changing her mind about Danny. If he helped this cow and brought her baby safely into the world, then he would be a hero in her eyes. The tricks he was playing with her and his son would be forgiven and forgotten.

After a few minutes there was still no sign of the calf being born. Maud was getting very anxious and didn't want to start the new year off with more sadness and possibly death even if it was that of an animal. Something came over her. Nobody was going to die on her watch. Not tonight. She looked the cow in the eyes and urged her to push.

"I know you're tired, baby. I know this blows, but Danny fixed it. It's OK. You can push now. *Push, baby, push! Please, baby, please push!*"

The guttural groan started up again. The cow's eyes rolled in her head.

At the cow's other end, Danny was egging her on. "*Come on, girl, atta girl! Good girl, you're a great girl, come on now!*"

And with that Maud heard the gush of the water and Danny's triumphant shout. It was out. Maud kissed the cow on her nose and held her face in hers for the longest time. The bells from St. Dominic's were ringing out. It was midnight and the new year had started. Not with death and sadness but with birth and hopefulness.

"Well done, Danny! That was totally awesome. Oh my God, totally awesome!"

"I don't know what you said to that cow but it surely did the job. I think you women know how to talk to each other alright. I don't know if she would ever have gone on if it was just me here," Danny said, washing his hands and arms in the soapy water he had brought out to the shed with him. "That's another one for the herd. A fine little heifer. If Tom ever comes home he'll have a fine number."

Maud didn't say anything. She knew by Tom's attitude on Christmas Eve that he had no intention of ever coming back to Inchahowen. But Danny could figure that one out for himself. It wasn't her place to hurt him with the truth.

She had a new respect for Danny, seeing the cow happily licking her baby girl.

"Come back to the kitchen and we'll raise a glass to our good work."

"It's late, Danny, I should go home."

"Go home to what? An empty house? A little drink won't do you a bit of harm."

Maud relented and went with Danny. He opened a bottle of whiskey and poured two glasses for them. Maud had sworn she would never drink again but tonight would be an exception. It wasn't every day that you helped to bring new life into the world.

As she wondered if her dad felt as high as this each time he safely delivered a newborn baby, Danny held out his glass to hers.

"*Sláinte, saol fada agus bás in Éireann!*" he said by way of a toast.

Maud didn't have a word of Irish but assumed that it was a friendly toast and didn't mean "get screwed" or anything like that. "What does that mean?" she asked.

"It means '*Health, a long life and may you die in Ireland!*'"

"Oh my god, that's some toast! *Sláinte!* Happy New Year," she said and took a sip. The whiskey warmed her throat and almost made her splutter. "You know what, Danny? You have made me very happy tonight. You may even have changed the way I look at my life, so thank you from the bottom of my heart."

"*Ara*, don't talk shite, girl. Just drink up."

Maud laughed so hard she thought she would fall off her chair and then Danny joined in. They laughed until they ran out of steam. After the laughter subsided, they sat in companionable silence finishing their drinks.

Danny went to pour more into Maud's glass but she put her hand over her glass. "Move your hand, lassie. Have one for the road. Or the ditch in your case."

Maud let him pour a small amount into her glass. She wanted to ask him about Tom. She wanted to know if he would ever come back and take up where he had left off with her.

"What's going on with you and Tom?" she asked. "Seems you really want him to come back and live here, *huh*?"

"I don't know if he will ever come back but, by God, I will die trying to make it happen. This is where he belongs."

Maud was sorry she had brought the subject up as it was making him sad.

"I don't mind saying he was closer to his mother than to me," Danny continued. "She was a beauty alright. She was a lot younger than me. Near twenty years younger. I never in my life thought I would get married. I resigned myself to being a bachelor and God knows I was content with my lot. I had the farm and I had some good neighbours. My brothers went to America but I never had to, you see. The farm was always going to be mine."

Maud sat back and listened to the story of Danny and Rose.

# Chapter Twenty

On the 31st of December 1968, Rose Traynor was to be married to PJ Harte. Rose and PJ had been going out together for ten years before PJ finally popped the question. As one of the two teachers in the tiny national school in Inchahowen, Rose's wedding was a big deal. The school children would be singing at the Mass and had been learning the songs for months in advance of the Big Day.

Rose was madly in love. She couldn't wait to finally be PJ's wife and start their own little family. Or big family. Rose wanted a big family, having no family of her own. Rose was from England originally and had no family in Ireland. She spent the morning getting ready in her own little house that she shared with her best friend Breda. PJ had arranged for all of her things to be brought to his house when they were in Wexford on their honeymoon.

Breda did Rose's hair and make-up and, when she was finished, Rose put on her wedding dress. It was a copy of a dress worn by Priscilla when she married Elvis. Rose had seen it in a magazine and when PJ proposed, she immediately set about getting a copy of the dress made. It was made of white satin and encrusted with pearls. She even had the same three-foot tulle veil. She was delighted with the result and felt like a million dollars as she got into the wedding car to go to the church.

But when they got to the church, Breda sensed something was wrong and got out of the car. She told Rose to stay where she was. The absence of the groom's wedding car hadn't registered with Rose. The guests who had been standing outside started to filter into the church.

Rose noticed PJ's brother Leo pull up into the church car park in his own car. She wondered why he hadn't travelled with the groom, still unaware that the groom's wedding car wasn't there. She saw Breda and Leo talking outside the door of the church. She started to get a bad feeling when the two of them simultaneously looked directly at her.

Breda got back into the car. Rose at that stage still unaware that her life was about to be turned upside-down.

"He's not here," Breda said.

"He's late, you mean?" said Rose.

"No, darling." Breda moved over in the back seat and took Rose in her arms.

"Mind my dress," protested Rose.

"He's gone to England. He's not coming back."

"What are you talking about? What are you ...?"

"He left a letter for Leo. And one for you. Here." Breda held out an envelope with Rose's name on it.

Rose opened the envelope, her hands shaking. She read the short note.

"*No!*" She let out a painful cry.

To Breda she sounded like a wounded animal.

"My angel!" Breda said, taking Rose in her arms.

Rose let herself sink into her friend's arms. How could he do this? How could he leave her at the altar? He could have told her. He could have said he wanted to wait another while. She had waited ten years already. She would have gladly waited another ten. She remembered the night before. She saw him for about five minutes. She was giddy with excitement but noticed that he seemed rather passive. She put it down to nerves. Not for a minute did she think it was because he didn't want to marry her.

"I want to go home," Rose said, sitting straight up in the car.

Breda instructed the driver to take them back to Rose's house.

⋙ ⋘

After being jilted at the altar, Rose became an object of pity in the village. In the immediate aftermath, she wanted to die. To disappear. But something inside her, a strength she didn't know she had, made her get up the following day and re-organise her life. She called to her landlord and told him that she would need to keep the lease on her house after all. She had organised to be on honeymoon during Easter holidays so she used the time she should have been in Wexford with PJ to good use. She returned gifts that they had received and wrote letters to each person thanking them for their kindness.

⋙ ⋘

In the years after, Danny spent more time than he needed to carrying out maintenance on the primary school in the village. He knew about Rose and PJ and he wondered how a man could do anything so brutal. Or how a man could be so stupid. Rose Traynor was the most lovely woman Danny had ever met. She was always polite to him but he never seemed to be able to get past initial pleasantaries with her, try as he might.

Danny knew she liked classical music and asked her if she'd like to go a concert in the City Hall in Cork with him. She politely declined his invite. He asked her if she wanted to go to see a film with him. She politely declined. Then, on a particularly hot day, he asked Rose if he could buy her an ice cream and was stunned when she said yes.

Danny and Rose started up a courtship. Neither were spring chickens. Danny was nearly forty and Rose was thirty-eight. It was ten years since PJ Harte broke Rose's heart but piece by piece Danny was beginning to put it back together. When Danny proposed a few months later, Rose accepted on the condition that they had a ceremony with only the two of them and a pair of witnesses. Although she knew Danny would not do what PJ did, she was still scarred from her previous experience.

After they were married, Rose moved into Danny's farmhouse and set about making the little house a home.

When Rose told Danny she was pregnant, he almost expired with happiness. He had never asked for a thing in his life and yet he was receiving all these bounteous blessings. He didn't know where it would end. Tom was born and he was the apple of their eyes and the source of their joy.

When Tom started school, Rose was his teacher. He was bright as a button and by the time he was six he could do sums and read like a twelve-year-old. Rose and Tom walked to and from school every day.

During school holidays, Tom spent time with Danny on the farm, hammering nails into fences and herding cattle. He was a strong little fella and they worked together in an amicable silence. Danny was slightly intimidated by his son, if truth be told. Rose and Tom would read at the kitchen table at night while Danny listened to programmes on the radio.

There was no doubt that Tom loved Danny but he adored Rose. They were like an extension of one another. It was hard to know where one person finished and the other began. Danny was envious of their close relationship but he was never jealous. Not once did he wish that he was the one sitting at the table with Tom. Never once did he resent their obvious mutual adoration.

One morning Rose woke, feeling unwell. She told Danny to take Tom to school and to let the other teacher know that she wouldn't be in and to get a sub if she could. Danny knew it had to be serious if Rose was taking the day off. She had never before missed a day. Danny dropped Tom to school and went straight back home. Rose was still in bed when Danny returned.

He knew immediately that she was gone when he entered the bedroom. It turned out she had a hole in her heart which was never picked up as a child because nobody had ever taken the trouble to check.

Tom took the blow on the chin. He missed his mother very much but he never acted out like Danny thought he would. In fact, Danny would have preferred if Tom had gone hysterical and vented his feelings a bit more.

Bit by bit, Danny and Tom started to adjust to life without Rose.

***

Danny finished his story and Maud's heart broke for the young motherless Tom. That poor boy who took his father's hand to bravely face the world without his mother grew into the handsome man who called to her door defending his father's rights.

Danny tried to pour another whiskey for Maud but this time she refused and left the house to cross the field to her own house. It was a cold night and she couldn't wait to get into her cosy bed.

# Chapter Twenty-One

The shop would be closed on New Year's Day and Maud was relieved that she didn't have to go to work. She relished the thought of the following day's lie-in. She let herself in her front door and delighted at the heat inside. She turned off the lights as she made her way up the stairs.

She brushed her teeth, cleaned her face and hopped into bed. The thought of the cow earlier on made her smile and she had a contented feeling that she hadn't felt in years. For the first time in a long time she looked forward to a new year that could be full of possibilities and promise even. Between the cow and the whiskey she was exhausted. She fell asleep straight away.

At some point during the night, she heard a noise downstairs. She sat bolt upright in the bed. For some strange reason she wasn't afraid of the noise. She got out of bed and put on her robe. She put the lights back on as she descended the stairs. There was a man sitting at her kitchen table with his back to her. She knew him straight away. She couldn't mistake her favourite brother Patrick, with his broad shoulders and short black hair.

She put her arm around his shoulders and pressed her cheek to his. He looked up and smiled at her. She was overjoyed to see him. She sat down next to him.

He was looking through a photograph album. It was opened on pages of pictures of Patrick Junior and Grace. There were also photographs of Martha and the children with John, Martha's new fiancé. They all looked so happy. How could they be happy without Patrick? Maud couldn't get over it, how could they? She didn't ask it in a judgemental way, she just didn't know how it was possible.

Her mom had brought the album to her as a present but Maud couldn't get up the nerve to open it. Her mom told her what photos the album contained but to Maud it contained only pain and guilt and she could not bring herself to look.

Patrick turned back to the beginning and they *ooohed* and *aaahed* over photographs of all of them as children in the big old house in Boston. She leaned into Patrick's big shoulder and felt comfort and peace there. He loved her still. He didn't blame her. It was not her fault. *It was not her fault.*

Maud woke up and stretched her long-legged body under the duvet. As she stretched, she remembered her dream. She had dreamt about

Patrick. She vividly recalled sitting at the table with him and feeling the warmth of his body beside her.

She got out of bed and went downstairs. She put ground coffee into a filter and pressed the button on the coffee machine. She was looking forward to a day lazing around in her PJs with nowhere to go and nobody to see. Every day the sea put on a show for her and today was no exception. The waves were huge and crashed onto the rocks in a crescendo of foam like a big white fireworks display. She congratulated herself again for choosing this great house to live in.

The coffee machine gurgled and she reached up to the cabinet to take out a mug. She poured  coffee and, turning around, noticed the photograph album open on the kitchen table. She had put it in the bookshelf when her mom gave it to her, unable to face the contents. How come it was now on the table? It was open on the page that she had seen in her dream with Patrick. The page of Martha, Patrick's wife, with her fiancé John and the children, all looking gloriously happy and complete.

She went back to the start and sure enough the faces of five little children like steps of stairs stared back at her. She had never looked through the album before but she knew each photograph it contained. She looked at each picture with tears streaming down her face, falling onto the pages and the faces of her family. She had shut herself off from all of them, thinking that they blamed her for Patrick's death but of course they didn't. She knew that now.

It had taken Patrick to come back from beyond the grave somehow to convince her that.

# Chapter Twenty-Two

Kate opened the door at seven o'clock. She had already been up for hours making cakes, hoping to entice the customers through the door with the delicious aromas. She loved her new shop and she was overjoyed and full of hope as she opened for business for the first time.

She was so grateful to Maud and she would repay her every cent with interest. The shop front was black with floor-to-ceiling windows on each side of the door. It was symmetrically perfect and it was no wonder that Kate and Maud had jumped at it when the estate agent showed it to them. The shop front was original and dated back to the 1920s when it was rebuilt after being bombed in the 1916 Rising. It had been a safe house for members of the Irish Republican Army and Kate loved that it had played some part in the history of the country.

It was a beautiful crisp January morning and the streets were still quiet. She had time to survey what she had created and she took time to smell the coffee which of course was freshly ground and from Aruba. Maud had insisted she stock this Fair Trade brand and Kate agreed because of her ravings about the quality and provenance. The aroma was amazing and hopefully it would draw in the passing punters. Kate felt a few pangs of panic rising but she pushed them back down. She decided not to entertain any negativity today of all days. Soon the first customer came through the door and it was showtime.

"Good morning," Kate said chirpily to the young man who was huddling, his coat clutched around him.

"Hi," was all he said as he looked around, taking in the wonderful surroundings.

Unlike the shopfront, the room was like a frilly confection. The bottom part of the walls were the original wood panelling and looked dark and inviting. Kate had chosen a candy-pink-and-white stripe for the top and the result gave off a vibe of quaint and modern at the same time.

The window display had two of the most fanciful cakes imaginable. She had iced three-foot-high Styrofoam shapes and the result was amazing. In one window there was a mock cake handbag. It was pink with black piping around the edges. The detail included pockets at the front of the bag. The fasteners and dangly key-chain were gold where Kate had turned the fondant gold with a food colouring. It would certainly stop passersby in their tracks, especially when they realised that she could make cakes to look like that.

The other window housed a three-foot-high stiletto shoe complete with red sole. The shoe was shiny black with a black-and-white bow. The Styrofoam was easier to work with than actual cake but Kate was confident that she could recreate the shoe in cake if she got an order for one. She was delighted with her window display and decided she would change it around every few days as she had worked for weeks to get the window display "cakes" ready. These were going to sell her cakes to the city and she had to make sure they had a big impact on the those passing by.

Kate had left space for only six tables, having given most of the space over to a big bakery in the back. The smells coming from there were divine. Even Mr. Grumpy First Customer started to loosen up a little when he got a waft of the baked goods. Kate had a selection of pastries on display and the young man had a hard time choosing.

"I'll have a coffee, please," he said to Kate. "Oh and I'll have a .. . a, *em*, a croissant. Sorry, everything looks so good."

"Thanks, I hope other people think so too. This is my first day."

"Oh, best of luck with it. I work around here but I've never noticed this place before. What did it use to be?"

She handed him his coffee and croissant. "To be honest, I don't know. I just know that it's my favourite shop in the world right now. Enjoy. Oh and it's on the house as you have the privilege of being my very first customer." She smiled at him.

"Thanks, that's very nice of you. I work up the street and I'll tell all my workmates about it." He smiled and went to a table at the window.

Kate wasn't sure but it seemed as if, as passersby saw him sitting there, the shop started to fill up.

Kate had asked Penny and Ingrid, her two new staff, to come in at eight as she wasn't sure how busy it would be. She was delighted to see them come in the door. They both ran upstairs quickly, changed into their aprons and got down to it straight away. Penny went in behind the counter and Ingrid started clearing tables.

These girls knew instinctively what to do and Kate thanked her lucky stars. It was b-u-s-y. From seven thirty the door never stopped opening. The original bell mechanism trilled all day. It sounded like something out of the Victorian era and Kate loved its chime. It meant traffic. Human traffic.

She noticed that, as in Inchahowen, when people settled in and had a coffee and a pastry, their demeanour changed for the better. People left happier than when they had come in. Kate imagined that they were more ready to face a day at the office, a boss they detested or a hard day trawling the shops. This job was going to be hard work, involving long hours and no social life but Kate thought: *Bring It On!*

By five o'clock the girls were shattered. It had been a lot busier than they had anticipated. By two o'clock they had sold out of all the cakes and pastries. Kate had to start baking, leaving Penny and Ingrid to look after the shop. It wasn't ideal as Kate wanted to meet and greet every single customer who came through her door. She would have to get up earlier the following morning to start baking for what hopefully would be another busy day at OTT Cakes.

⤛⤜

Before the first week was out, Kate knew exactly what the word *exhaustion* meant. Even muscles she didn't know she had ached. But somehow adrenalin had made the pain bearable. She worked every day from early mornings to late in the evenings and had Sunday off as she was aware that even she could not work twenty-four hours a day, seven days a week and three-hundred-and-sixty-five days a year.

On her first Sunday off she made the mistake of standing in her empty shop and watching all the people pass the door, counting up in her head how much a small percentage of those passing would spend if she were open for business. But her sensible head told her that she wouldn't be open for business for long if she didn't take a day to recharge her overworked batteries.

⤞⤙

For the first few months, Kate and Maud met over Zoom once a week to go over figures and projections. Kate valued the time Maud gave to her and was astounded anew that a woman who possessed so much knowledge and wisdom was happy to run a coffee shop in a tiny seaside village in West Cork.

She had broached the subject once more but Maud just brushed her off, saying that being in Inchahowen suited her perfectly, and was just what she needed in her life right now. Kate knew not to push her any more for the moment.

Kate hoped that Maud's new role as her investor and mentor wouldn't mean that their friendship would have to suffer as a consequence. Maud forensically went through Kate's figures and Kate was nervous despite herself. Maud was intimidating at these weekly meetings even if they were virtual.

"It doesn't look like you have many cake orders. Are you concentrating on this? I thought this was to be the main business," Maud said, looking up from the stack of printouts she had been looking at.

"I've been concentrating on getting open and pastries, but I know that I need to advertise the cakes. I've got signs up in the shop but I've only received two orders so far. The feedback was amazing but I know I need to get cracking on getting more orders."

"*Mmmm...*"

Maud looked worried and the last thing Kate wanted was a worried Maud. She explained what she had done to attract corporate business so far.

"That kind of business is not going to come walking in your door. You're going to have to go out and get it. For now, you're doing fine – you're paying the bills, you're keeping the doors open. But you gotta think big, Kate, go for the big fish. They're the ones who would think nothing of paying thousands of euro for an enormous cake for an event. They'll have all the media coverage too. I suggest you bake cakes related to their business activities and drop them off to every GM or MD of every big company in the city. It'll cost but, oh boy, the rewards you reap will be worth it. Don't worry, it'll work. I'm sure of it."

Kate wanted to kick herself for not coming up with this idea herself. Maud could see the thought crossing her face.

"You know, Kate, I didn't know everything when I started out. In fact, I knew very little but I learned as I went. And so will you. Don't look so worried, I'm here to help."

"I know and I am really grateful that you take time out for this every week. And that you're always at the end of the phone for me. I'm frustrated that I'm not where I should be in terms of sales. I'm being impatient, that's all."

"You're doing great. The first phase, the coffee shop, is doing well. Now it's time for the corporate bit. One step at a time."

But Kate had other reasons to worry. She hadn't told Maud the whole story. She had needed to take on extra staff to cover some of the shifts in OTT. There were too many hours in the week and not enough of Kate, Ingrid and Penny to go around.

She had extra costs with wages and she also hadn't told Maud the full extent of the money she owed to creditors. She was in over her head and she was starting to panic. Even though they had negotiated on the rent, the cost was still enormous. She knew that the advice Maud gave her about the ways to promote her business made sense but she just didn't know how she would pay for it. She needed to get exposure some other way and she needed it soon.

# Chapter Twenty-Three

"Simon York on line one," Tom's assistant Anna buzzed through.

Tom picked up. "Simon, thanks for getting back to me."

"No! Thank *you*, Tom. I think you've just given me the story of the year. Well, I know it's only January but you know what I mean!"

"OK, I'm waiting. Am I going to like what you have to say?"

"Well, it's nothing to do with the trials of this new drug. It looks like Gilbrade are moving to Asia – lock, stock and barrel. In a nutshell, they have shut down or are phasing out all European and North American operations and are shifting all development and production to South Korea."

"Go on," Tom urged him.

"They seem to have moved all funds to South Korea already. They have no assets or cash on their balance sheet because it's all in a new company they formed called Gilbrade Pharma Asia. It's perfectly legal. They paid off all their staff, offered to relocate those who wanted to go and shut up shop."

"What were they going to do with Belfast? Why bother to start to build it at all if they were just going to up sticks and leave? I don't understand."

"It was purely a distraction. A decoy, if you will. While the stock market and people in the industry took it that they were expanding their European operations, they were stealthily moving all of their production and monies to South Korea. Seoul is now their place of interest for trading purposes."

"What can I do about any of this?" Tom groaned. "I mean, I'm going to have to shut up shop myself and let all my people go soon!"

"You need to get your team of lawyers on to them immediately. I'll be running a story on this as soon as I have all the facts and I'll run it by our own legal department. I'm hoping to use your name and your firm as examples of multi-nationals running amok – if that's alright with you?"

"Yes, I suppose it is. I'll have to brief all the staff today. I'll call a meeting and tell them what I know so far and try to reassure them, I suppose," said Tom, knowing a story in *Business Weekly* couldn't do him any harm at this juncture.

He thanked Simon for filling him in and arranged to meet him the following day to discuss his deal with Gilbrade over lunch.

Tom reluctantly called all of his staff together to break the bad news to them. Some of them had been with him from the beginning and some of them had even become friends.

He looked around at the faces gathered in the boardroom and he felt truly humble. He was responsible for the livelihoods of all of these people. They had husbands and wives, children and mortgages and lifestyles which they funded by working with Tom. It weighed heavily on his conscience and he owed it to each one of them to be as truthful as he could be.

Gilbrade had looked like a goose that would lay the golden egg, but it was turning out to be the golden bomb exploding right here in the boardroom. Tom had travelled the world with a team of architects and engineers, looking at state-of-the-art pharmaceutical production facilities, and had drawn up and designed a state-of-the-art facility that had no equivalent anywhere else on earth.

They had put their hearts, souls and profits into making the Gilbrade Belfast facility the best in the world and this had to count for something. The faces of his staff when he told them was something that Tom would not forget for a long time. The shock turned to horror but then turned to something else: bloody determination. They were all in agreement that they had done nothing to deserve this cruel twist of fate.

Tom's confidence was boosted by their defiance and their collective conviction that the company would survive.

***

Tom was exhausted and flicked off his computer. He couldn't look at the figures or the problems any more. He wanted a drink but decided against it. Drink would fudge his thoughts and he was meeting Simon tomorrow. He wanted his brain to be in top gear. He wanted to pick up on and understand everything that Simon told him and he also wanted to give a clear and concise interview in return.

It was nine o'clock and the building in Canary Wharf was empty now. He had designed this building himself and he leased one floor from his client to set up his offices. He got the lift down to the ground floor and said goodnight to the security guys.

God, he was tired. Maybe this was the natural end. Maybe this was the way things were intended. He had been so wrecked lately and was even feeling the influence his father was having on him and thinking that maybe it wouldn't be the worst thing in the world to go back to Inchahowen.

He was obviously having some kind of meltdown. His life was in London now. Molly was here, and he would never leave his daughter. Anyway, what the hell would he do looking at cows all day on the rugged Atlantic shore?

He felt bad for being so hard on his old man. He wasn't a bad man in any way, just lonely. Danny had been the one to encourage Tom to leave in the first place. Tom would have stayed – in fact, he almost didn't have the strength to leave his father behind. He remembered the conversation as if it was yesterday.

"You're going, son, and that's all about it. Your mother would have wanted you to go. You know what she was like about school. She wanted you to have all the chances that a good education can offer."

"But what about you, Dad? What are you going to do? How will you manage on the farm? Who will take care of you?"

"What do you think I am? A feckin' baby? Jesus Christ, boy, I was looking after meself long before you came along and I will look after meself long after you go too. Look after me, is it? Feck sake!" Danny was angry now.

"OK, but I hope you're sure cos when I'm gone, the chances are I won't be coming back."

"Maybe not now but someday you will. You have to go and live the life your mother would have wanted you to live. Make her proud."

The two men embraced and both had tears in their eyes which they hid from each other.

Tom went off to university to study architecture and moved to London when he graduated. He got a job working for a big architectural firm. He spent a few years leaning all he could from them and then decided to start his own company.

He knew that Danny was proud of him. His father had press clippings of every building Tom ever designed and kept them in a scrapbook which was in a drawer of the dresser in the cottage in Inchahowen.

Tom knew that in his father's eyes he was the best thing since sliced bread. Tom was finding it very difficult to live up to his father's idea of him right at this moment. What would Danny say if he knew that he was in danger of losing everything he had worked for? Knowing his father, he would side with him, his son. As far as Danny was concerned, he could do no wrong. When his marriage to Valerie broke down, Danny didn't lecture or make any judgement though Tom had expected him to be disappointed that he couldn't make his marriage work.

"She was a bit of an oul' shnob anyway – you'll be better without her if you ask me," was all he said.

Tom knew his father needed to take the blinkers off. He wasn't perfect. Far from it. But Danny would never see that.

⋙ ⋘

Tom had wanted to be an architect from as far back as he could remember. Living in a tiny village, he never saw high rise buildings or any building that wasn't a farm building, house or shop. As a child on their rare trips to Dublin he was fascinated by the tall buildings, which in reality weren't that tall at all. He spent all his time there looking up and as a result bumping into people on the wide city streets. His father would grab his hand and tell him to pay attention to where he was and not be looking into space.

One summer he met some boys, brothers, from Boston who were on holidays in Inchahowen. Tom became obsessed with the lads. Not only because they had great fun playing in the dunes on the beach or exploring the woods but because they were from the city with the big skyscrapers. Tom wished he could go back to the States with them at the end of the summer. Not for good but just to see the buildings and to experience their grandeur from the streets.

# Chapter Twenty-Four

Danny sat in his armchair beside the fire. The television was on but it was just noise in the background until the news came on at nine o'clock. It was lonely living on his own with just the television for company. But he was luckier than most because he could walk to the pub. The lads from the back of beyond couldn't do that.

On rare days he wouldn't see a single soul from one end of the day to the other. He had eaten his tea at six just like he did every evening, winter and summer. Mrs. Pierce made dinners for him and put them in the little freezer compartment in his fridge. The meals on wheels came twice a week with a dinner for him and he ate it at one o'clock on the button. He was a creature of habit and there was no chance he was going to change in his eightieth year.

He got up at seven every morning and had his breakfast before going out to walk the land and check the cattle. He noticed lately that the American lass came in on her way to work and cleaned up the kitchen for him. She was a nice girleen. He was sorry that his attempts to get her together with Tom hadn't worked out. All in all, though, it had been worth a go. She was a good-looking girl too. Strong as well and not afraid of hard work. He liked that in a person. He had taken to calling into the coffee shop in the middle of the morning to have a – what do you call it now? A cappuccino. It was only a fancy name for coffee but it tasted lovely all the same.

His thoughts then turned to Valerie. She was a right pain in the hole. A pure snob. Tom got notions about himself in London, and now Danny feared his son might be turning into a bit of a snob as well. God help us! It was far from that shite he was reared. Danny made the trip to London for the wedding. Jesus, but he couldn't wait to get home out of it. How Tom wanted to stay there he would never know. The noise was in his head for days after he came back to Inchahowen!

On their occasional visits, Valerie used to hold her nose to block out the smell of the farm. A good natural smell like that – Jesus wept! And Molly, the poor little divil. It was a pity for her and a pity for Tom that he would be separated from his own child, but he hoped that they would be sensible enough to work something out that suited the wee one.

Molly never held her nose when she came to visit, which wasn't very often, mind you. She would sit on Danny's knee and he would tell her stories about when her daddy was a little boy and show her around the farm and let her feed the lambs and calves. She was a ticket and he hoped that she wouldn't grow up to be too like her mother.

He had the feeling that he wouldn't be seeing Tom for a while. He was very annoyed when he left after Christmas to go back to London. Danny really did feel a pain in his chest on Christmas Eve. He wouldn't have asked Tom to come all the way if he hadn't thought it was serious. He had felt the tightening in his chest and he got a fright. He took an aspirin just like Doctor O'Neill had told him to and he lay down. He slept and when he woke up the pain was gone.

Tom didn't believe him, he could tell. Tom normally was patient and kind but this time was different. Maybe he and Valerie were fighting about something or other but he surely wasn't his usual self. But the main thing was that he came. He came, God bless him! He wouldn't call him again though – he wouldn't do that to him again. He'd have to be dead to tell him to come home the next time.

# Chapter Twenty-Five

Tom met with his lawyers at their offices on Chancery Lane. They were involved in the drawing up of the contract Tom had entered into with Gilbrade and were up to speed by the time Tom met with them.

"What do you suggest as a course of action?" he asked.

"We will have to establish that they knowingly engaged your company's services though they never had any intention of completing the project. We would also have to try to prove that they used the building of the facility in Belfast as a cover, pretending that it was business as usual when in fact they were moving assets and personnel to Asia," Doug aka Douglas Bennett QC said to his client. "Tom, this is in no way a cut-and-dried case. Gilbrade have millions of pounds to throw at this. They could bankrupt you in the process and indeed that is probably the tactics they will try to employ. They will drag this out until you have to throw in the towel. As soon as we serve any sort of writ on them, they will delve into your company history and your private life to see what they think you will be able to withstand. They will go back and review every set of accounts Kennedy Architects has filed since the year dot, together twith your assets and pounce on any weakness they perceive is there."

Doug left that bit hanging in the air. He didn't want Tom to be under any false illusions. He could lose everything here and he needed to understand that.

"But do you think I have a case? Do you think I should take them on? That's what I'm here to find out," Tom asked squarely.

"I think morally you have a case, yes. But the technicalities are crucial here. Was there a clause in the contract to cover you if it all went belly-up? It's vague and I couldn't possibly give you the answer you're looking for. Gilbrade's legal team will have gone over this already and one thing you can be sure of is that they're satisfied *they* don't have anything to worry about."

This wasn't playing out the way Tom wanted it to. It seemed he would have a hard job standing up to Gilbrade and Doug wasn't being optimistic about his chances. But Tom felt such an overwhelming feeling of being wronged that he couldn't let it go. He couldn't turn around to all of his employees and his friends and tell them all that it was great working with them, great getting to know them all and their families but that it was over. The company was over. He had been screwed over by a giant pharmaceutical company and he was walking away defeated. No way. He was going to have a go at them no matter what the cost to him was personally. The bank had agreed to float him for another three months to cover salaries and some expenses but they had made it clear that they would not be willing to make money available to him for his legal fees without some sort of security.

Tom knew that Valerie would not agree to mortgaging the house in Notting Hill. He wouldn't even ask her anyway. It was Molly's home and to him that was sacred. One thing kept creeping up from the back of his mind. Danny had sent him the deeds of the land in Inchahowen last year. When he got the envelope in the post that day Tom rang his father asking what he wanted him to do with them.

"I bought the land for you. You're my son and heir. I won't be around forever so I want you to have it. I signed it all over to you in my will the other day."

"Dad, you'll probably outlive me. I'll send them back to you." Tom didn't want to be having this conversation.

"You will do nothing of the sort. Keep them. They're yours. There's a right load of land there, son. I was buying whatever came up for sale over the years. There's one hundred and fifteen acres altogether. There's a few houses on the land too. You'd make a fine job of some of them, no doubt. Though there's some of them only fit for the bulldozer."

Tom was blown away by his father's revelations. One hundred and fifteen acres. He was a dark horse. Tom wasn't sure what valuations for agricultural land was currently but the farmland was surely worth a small fortune.

"Thanks, Dad." Although the words were inadequate, it was all he could say.

"I want you do something with the land, son. Something that'd be good for everyone."

"I will, Dad. I'll make sure of it," said Tom, though he had no idea at that stage what he would do.

What would Danny think about him using the deeds as security for a loan to take on Gilbrade in Court? He had never discussed his problems with his father because he didn't want to worry him. No, that wasn't the reason. He didn't want Danny's high opinion of him to change, he wanted him to continue to think he was the greatest thing on two legs.

Tom argued back and forth with himself and wrestled with his conscience, wondering if it was the right thing to do. It ended with the realisation that it was the only thing he could do. Hopefully Danny would never even know a thing about it, he told himself. If he won the case, that was.

He made the call to Doug.

"Doug, I can get the money. I want to do this. I have to do this. Start preparing and serve them as soon as possible."

"If you're sure. You'll need a strong stomach for it. We have to tear their reputation to shreds. It's a long shot. And it could cost maybe a hundred thousands pounds."

"I have no choice. Serve them as soon as you're prepared. The sooner the better."

Tom was scared shitless by his decision to use the deeds to borrow money to fight Gilbrade. He felt like he had just walked into the bookies and put the money on a horse.

He was rewarded by not being able to get thoughts of his father out of his mind for the rest of the day. Tom loved Danny but they were both the type of man who found it hard to express his feelings. They were both sure that the other knew he loved him but they never found the courage to say it to each other. Tom knew that he would probably benefit from sitting on a psychotherpasist's couch for a day or two but he never could find the time to do it.

He was pretty much fucked. He didn't have a wife anymore and his daughter was now from a broken home. His business was in dire straits and he was risking the fortune that Danny had spent his life building up for him.

# Chapter Twenty-Six

Kate had created a monster. A monster that took up all her time, creativity and energy. She had nothing spare to give to any other pursuit. She ate, drank and slept the cake shop. But she still wasn't able to pay off the creditors at the end of every month. She really needed Maud's expertise now but she couldn't reveal the extent of how far she had let things go. She had received a threatening phone call the evening before from a supplier and it still made her shudder when she thought of the tone of the conversation.

"Sorry, love, but you still owe me tree hundred and forty euros. I'll give you one more week, righ? Then you'll owe me five hundred euros and a week after tha' you'll owe me a tousand. Do ya geddit? One more week and I want every single penny. Otherwise, I'll have to go into your lovely cake shop and take your stuff to pay for it. And we don't want that now, do we?"

She could hear the threat in his voice and she knew for sure he meant what he said. He would strip out her mixers and anything else of value to pay his outstanding bill. *Shit*. How did she let herself get into this mess? Maud had offered her more start-up money but she had stupidly insisted that she didn't need any more money. No, sir!

The super-duper Miss Kate Harrington would open a cake shop in the centre of Dublin on a shoestring and be an amazing success! What the hell was she thinking? She needed her head examined and she needed to come up with the money in the next few days.

Kate looked around the bustling shop. In different areas of the kitchen there were people baking, shaping, shaving and assembling cakes. In the front area, there was the constant hum of people in and out the door getting their coffees and pastries. The bell buzzed constantly from the time she opened her doors until she shut up shop at seven each evening. So why were the figures not adding up? She had a few long nights ahead of her trying to pinpoint where the heck all the money was going.

She knew her staff were expensive but she needed great bakers, it was an essential element of the grand master plan to be the best cake shop in Dublin. There was a lot of training involved but she was satisfied that they were all up to standard by now. The recipes were drilled into each baker and they knew not to stray from her clear concise instructions.

Depending on the design and size, each cake could require five different cakes to make it. There were requests for tiers to be different flavours so everyone was kept on their toes and had to concentrate fully on the job at hand. Despite the pressure they were under, they all enjoyed what they were doing and there was a great buzz in the bakery. They all felt that they were part of something new and something that was about to take Dublin by storm.

Kate contacted her friend Maeve who she had worked with at Ireland Telecom. Maeve was the PR manager and knew everyone in the media in Dublin. Maeve was thrilled to hear from her old pal and was only too happy to meet her for lunch the following day.

⤜⤜⤜ ⤛⤛⤛

"Kate, it's so good to see you," Maeve said as she gave her a hug. "I was sorry to hear your dad passed away. I'm terrible, I didn't even go to the funeral but you know it's hard to get out of work, things are so crazy."

"That's OK. I wouldn't expect you to drive all that way. I got your card and letter and I really appreciated it. How are you? You look great. Just like a successful business woman should look."

"I do in my arse," Maeve said and both girls laughed.

Kate was happy to see that the corporate lifestyle hadn't eroded Maeve's down-to-earth personality.

"So ... tell me all about OTT Cakes. I'm a lover of everything OTT so I'm dying to get to see it and taste some of the goods."

The girls spent a couple of hours catching up properly and bitching about the same people they bitched about when they worked together. Kate was grateful to be having a normal conversation. To be talking about things other than cake. She had been so completely consumed by cake and icing sugar since she arrived in Dublin that she forgot there was any other life happening out there.

"So what can I do to help you, Kate?"

"Well, I would love it if you could pull in a favour with somebody in the newspapers' lifestyle mags. I could really do with the free publicity. My budget is kinda, well, non-existent really. I really need the cakes to be photographed and spread over a few glossy pages. Food porn if you will!"

They both laughed.

"I get you. I know Justine Byrne who is editor of *Star Magazine*. She did a feature on *moi* last year sometime. Well, it wasn't just me, it was a woman in business article and she was really lovely to deal with. She kinda champions women and their enterprises. I'll call her and give her the lowdown on you. Should I give her your mobile so that she can contact you directly?"

"Maeve, you're a star yourself! Yes, give her my number of course. How will I ever thank you?"

"Hold your horses, nothing has happened yet. But if it does, I will expect my reward in cake."

"You've got a deal. You can stop by and eat your body weight in chocolate fudge cake."

# Chapter Twenty-Seven

Kate got back to her beautiful shop and Ingrid told her that a Mick Flynn had called. He left a message to say that he would be back at eight o'clock to get what she owed him. Kate felt a chill running down her spine. This could be the end of the line for OTT if she didn't do something about it.

She would pay the money. She wanted to pay him. She just needed some more time. She had been up nights poring over the figures and the penny finally dropped. No credit-card sales had been credited to her by her bank. She had called the bank and they had been very apologetic but they would not be able to correct their error until the following week. Kate tried to explain that she needed the funds credited straight away but to no avail. She asked them for an overdraft on her overdraft but they said that it would also take a few days to process her request. After f'ing and blinding for a few minutes, she decide that her bank manager was well and truly off her Christmas card list.

She knew it was pointless but she picked up the phone anyway and dialled Mick's number. She tried to explain but she might as well have been talking Japanese to him. He wanted his money and he wanted it now. Kate wondered why she ever did business with him but then remembered that he was way cheaper than any of the other suppliers. Cheap in the short term might be about to cost her everything.

She wanted to kick herself for being so naïve. When something seemed too good to be true, it normally was. When she thought back, all of the other suppliers had asked her to sign credit agreements and had asked for references. Not Mick, he just wanted to be paid in cash. She hadn't known that he would demand his money when he felt like it.

She hadn't signed any contract with him so he could do business on whatever terms he wanted to. She knew now that she was a victim of some sort of racketeer. She wanted to go to the police but she knew deep down that it wouldn't do any good. Mick would come and wreck the place when there was no one around.  He would always be over her shoulder with his hand out looking for money. Even if she paid him what she owed him and never did business with him again, he would never go away. He would see her as an easy touch.

A woman on her own, she was an easy target for a scumbag like him. She needed to get Mick Flynn out of her life. She didn't know anybody in Dublin who could help her so she had to make a phone call back to Inchahowen.

"Hi, it's me. I need your help," Kate said simply.

"What? You don't know how to get the stick out of your arse?" said Emer, not sounding thrilled to be hearing from her sister.

"I'm in trouble," said Kate.

"Ha!" Emer couldn't hide her satisfaction. "What kind of trouble?"

"There's a guy who's threatening me. I owe him money and he's coming to the shop to take my stuff if I don't give him what I owe him."

"Kate? Is that you for real? Are you messing?" said Emer, not believing her own ears. This was the last phone call she thought she would ever get. Perfect Kate with the perfect life needed her help! Perfect Kate who couldn't get away from them all quickly enough.

"Yes, I am for real. You know I wouldn't call you unless, well, you know ... I hate asking you for anything but this guy is going to wreck my gorgeous shop. I won't have the money for him until next week. There was a mix-up with the bank but he doesn't want to hear any of that. He wants his money and he wants it tonight. If he takes any of my stuff, I won't be able to operate. It will ruin me." Kate was pleading to her sister's better nature, not sure that she even had one.

"So what has any of that got to do with me? You've got a bit of a nerve ringing me, you know. You never bother to ask how Kylie is. Your own bloody niece and you couldn't give a shite about her. The same for Grace. And then you just ring out of the blue when you're in trouble. I bet I won't hear from you when you're about to make your first million!" Emer was getting plenty of pent-up anger off her chest.

Kate had expected as much. She had walked away from her sisters and hadn't looked back. From her fresh perspective, she saw that they were victims of their upbringing and they just weren't lucky enough or smart enough to break the cycle like she did.

She would try to make amends whether they helped her or not. The three of them needed to sit down and thrash it all out. They were all angry and they were all scarred by their childhoods. She hoped that

Emer and Grace would be able to overcome the past and make good lives for themselves. But that was all for another day. Today she needed them to put the past aside.

"I need some men to be here when that guy arrives. I think this guy might be dangerous. In fact, I'm sure of it. I don't want them to hurt anybody, just to explain to him that I will have the money next week and to, *em*, persuade him that it's better if he waits for the money and not take any of my equipment. I was thinking that Haystack and Doc would be able to persuade anybody to do anything really."

Haystack and Doc were her sisters' boyfriends. They were tough as nails with an appetite for danger. They were the perfect men for the job. They wouldn't run away in fear from Mick the supplier, and Mick, if he had any sense, would run a mile when he saw them in the shop.

Haystack was so called because of his straw-blond hair and his physique which was short and wide. He was as strong as an ox and Kate remembered when he had offered to beat the living daylights out of their father on their behalf until the girls talked him down. Their father had spent the day drinking as usual and was kicking up a fuss about his dinner being cold when he eventually came home from the pub.

Doc was the exact opposite of Haystack physically but he was wiry and strong. He had taken on almost everyone who wanted a fight in Inchahowen and won. Kate couldn't believe she was actually inviting these characters into her new life but she couldn't think of a better alternative.

"For fuck's sake, Kate. Doc and Haystack? I never remember you having a good word to say about either of them. And now you want them to come to your rescue? I'll tell you what, you've got a bigger pair of balls than the pair of them put together." Emer was amazed at her sister's request.

"Look, Emer, I don't have much time. I need them to be here by seven-thirty this evening." She reckoned Mick was likely to come ahead of time in case she scarpered. "I know you don't like me. I know I've no right to ask you for anything but I'm begging you. I swear I'll make it up to you. I know we have our problems, I know all that – but, for now, please help me. *Please.*"

"I'll ring you back in five minutes," Emer said and hung up the phone.

Kate flopped down into a chair and put her head in her hands. *This is not going to be the end. This is not going to be the end.* She kept repeating this mantra over and over until her phone buzzed in her hands.

"Well?" she asked.

"They'll do it but they want to know what they're going to get in return."

More like Emer was wondering what they would get, thought Kate. The lads would probably have done it for nothing as causing trouble and getting into fights was the way they got their kicks.

"I'll pay them a hundred euro each and cover all of their expenses," said Kate, hoping that would swing it.

"Deal," said Emer.

Kate was surprised that her sister didn't try to haggle.

Emer gave her Haystack's number. Her heart was thumping in her chest. She rang him to give him directions to the shop. She explained to Haystack that she thought these guys were dangerous but she couldn't be sure just how dangerous. Haystack understood exactly what she was saying and told her not to worry about anything. He had a hunting licence and a few nice pieces which would scare the living shite out of anybody. He assured her that he had no fear of anyone and she began to breathe normally for the first time in days.

# Chapter Twenty-Eight

She closed up the shop as usual at seven that evening and tried to rush the staff out the door. She didn't want them to see Haystack or Doc when they arrived. She knew what she was doing was very risky and she didn't want to incriminate any of her employees. She also didn't want Mick going after any of them. This was her mess and she needed to clean it up.

At twenty past seven there was a loud banging at the back door and she jumped even though she was expecting it. She opened up to see the old faces from her old life. She shook hands with them awkwardly but how else did you greet men, one of whom got your sister pregnant, and who you were asking to threaten someone on your behalf?

"How'r'ya, Kate?" said Haystack.

"How'r'ya?" said Doc.

"Thanks for coming so quickly," was all she could say in spite of what she had asked them to do.

"Sure we only hit the road in shpots!" said Doc and Kate believed him. They used to be boy racers back in the day so they must have enjoyed the few hours on the open road.

She led them into the back of the shop where they dropped their gearbags. She gasped when they started to take rifles and handguns out. *Oh my God*, she thought. *What have I got myself into?* She hadn't been sure if Mick and his thugs would have guns but she'd been sure if they had they wouldn't be as big or as numerous as the ones the two men were taking out of their bags. Kate felt sick and thought she was going to throw up. She wanted to tell them that it had been a mistake, to pack up their guns and go home ... but she needed them.

This was the game she was in at the moment, thanks to her own stupidity. And maybe she wouldn't need them after all. Maybe Mick would listen to reason and wait until next week. Maybe she was wrong about him being a thug. And maybe pigs could fly, she thought.

She gave them coffee and cake and they were sitting down against the wall stuffing plates of cakes into their mouths like it was the most natural thing in the world to be in a cake shop in Dublin waiting to frighten the living daylights out of a hardened criminal. She told them to stay in the back – that she would first try again to reason with Mick.

The banging on the door came soon after and Kate saw Doc and Haystack grab their guns and ready themselves. She looked back at them as she went to answer the door.

"Where's the dosh, love?" Mick said without preamble, pushing past her with a sidekick in tow.

"I told you, Mick, I won't have the money until next week. If you would just wait till then I'll be able to pay you everything."

"Nah, love. You'll never pay me evertin'. You'll always owe me sometin', that's how it works, see? The price is gone up now, did I tell ya? It's gone up to a tousand."

"A thousand? What the hell are you talking about? I owe you three-hundred and forty and I'll give it to you on Friday. Now get the hell out of my shop or I'll call the Gardaí." She was hoping the threat of involving the police would work and that Doc and Haystack could be on their merry way back to West Cork.

"Ah no, love. You won't ring the cops. No, to be fair to you, we'll just take your stuff tonight and then you can pay me the tousand on Friday. I'm bein nice now, so count yerself lucky."

Mick and his thug buddy started to unplug her coffee machine and knocked over the cups and mugs that were alongside it. They were going to destroy her business and she was relieved that she had called in some back-up.

At the sound of the breaking cups, Doc and Haystack appeared in front of Mick like his worst nightmare. Doc shouted at Kate to get in the back and she did what she was told but couldn't resist peeping out. Haystack had the barrel of a shotgun in Mick's face and was screaming at him. The other thug was being held by Doc and had a small handgun pointed at his groin. She imagined that he was having a hard time keeping his bladder in check. Kate couldn't believe that this scene was taking place in her little cake shop. She nervously listened to the conversation that Haystack was having with Mick.

"I'm going to be a permanent fixture here now, boy. If I ever see your face around here again, I'm going to follow you and I am going to shoot your ugly fucking head off. *Am I making meself clear? Can you understand me alright?*" he said, right in Mick's face.

"*You fucking culchie bollix!*" Mick spat back at him.

"I tell ya what. I'll blow the fucking Dublin bollix off you while I'm at it. *Do you fucking understand me?* You come near this shop or near this woman again and you are a fucking dead man with no bollix!"

"I'll come back when you're not here. You better tell her to watch her back because  someday I'll be righ' behind her ready to get her," said Mick, unable to give in.

Haystack pushed the barrel further into Mick's forehead and Kate imagined that he would have the imprint of the gun there for a long time.

"I will fucking shoot you right now, you fucker! I am giving you a chance to do the decent thing and fuck off. I'll give you five seconds to make your mind up. I will bury your body somewhere so remote that you'll never be found. I'm a mad fucker, me. I've done it before and I'll do it again. So five seconds. *Five. Four. Three. Two …*"

"Alrigh', alrigh'. I swear I'll leave her alone. I'll never come back here again."

"Good move. Now get the fuck out of here before I set the dogs on yiz!" said Haystack, pulling open the door.

Then he and Doc threw the men out into the street. They stood watching Mick and sidekick  take off down the street, then Doc slammed the door and locked it.

Kate came out from the back as her protectors high-fived, grinning. She was trying to get her breathing back to normal. She had never witnessed anything as violent as that in her whole life – but she was grateful to the men who had come to her rescue.

"Oh my God! Thank you so much. *Thank you*. Do you really think he's gone for good?" she said.

"I fucking well would be if it was me," said Doc.

"Did you really bury somebody before?" Kate asked Haystack.

"Not at all, but sure 'tis no harm to put the fear of God in him."

Kate was relieved that he hadn't. She wouldn't be comfortable with her niece's father being a murderer.

"Jaysus, I'm starvin'!" piped up Doc. "I'd murder a MacDonald's, is there one nearby?"

"That's enough talk of murder for one night!" Kate laughed nervously. "What if they come back though? Seriously, do you think they won't?"

"I'm telling you this for nothing," said Haystack. "If I just went through what those fellas did, I wouldn't be seen dead around here again. I think you can forget about Mick Whatever-his-name-is bothering you again."

Kate breathed a sigh of relief, though still not convinced that her ordeal was over. "Thanks a million, fellas. I mean I ... I ... Thanks very much."

"You're grand," said Doc. "Sure we're practically family. Now where's that MacDonald's?"

# Chapter Twenty-Nine

Maud was walking to work and called into Danny's house on the way as she had been doing for months now. He was usually out tending to the animals and she tidied things away for him and checked the presses and the fridge to see if there was anything he was running low on.

Mrs. Pierce was still the main person who looked after him but Maud thought the more people looking after him, the better. Mrs. Pierce didn't normally call until lunchtime anyway so she was grateful to Maud for having the place tidy. This morning things seemed a bit different.

The table hadn't been used and the kitchen was neat and tidy. Maud shouted down the house for him but Danny didn't answer. She didn't want to intrude on his privacy so she hesitated before checking the bedrooms.

Then she heard Ned whining upstairs. She went up and found Danny lying on the floor in his room. He was barely breathing and unconscious. His pulse was so faint it was hardly there. She rang for an ambulance and Doctor O'Neill. The doctor arrived on the scene within a few minutes. He had been on his way to the surgery and diverted to Danny's house.

He gave him an injection and got his pulse back to a more healthy rate. The ambulance arrived and took him to the hospital. Danny had had a heart attack. Maud felt she should follow the ambulance to the hospital. Somebody needed to be with Danny.

She locked Ned in the house as he seemed distressed and she feared he might follow the ambulance.

She rang Mrs. Pierce and asked her to contact Tom in London. Maud was glad that she didn't have to make that call as she imagined it wouldn't be met with a very favourable response and wondered if he would even come at all. She told her that Ned was locked in the house and Mrs. Pierce assured her that the dog would be looked after. Danny would want to be sure of that.

⤞⤝

Maud spent the day sitting outside the Intensive Care Unit watching the doctors and nurses going in and out. They didn't give her much information as she wasn't a relative.

Maud had called the coffee shop and Eva, her new assistant, told her that she had everything in hand. Eva was very capable and a good baker but nothing like Kate. She didn't possess any of Kate's finesse or creativity.

Towards the end of the long day, one of the nurses asked Maud if she'd like to sit with Danny for a few minutes. Maud went into the ICU. The nurse pulled back the curtain to allow Maud in. Danny looked so small in the bed, hooked up to machines. She sat beside him and put her hand on his. She reassured him that he was going to be fine, that he was going to be home in Inchahowen in no time. But she wasn't convinced.

A few seconds later, Maud felt Danny squeezing her hand. Not a tight squeeze but a certainly some kind of movement of his muscles. She called the nurses straight away who seemed to take it as a good sign. She kept talking to him, certain that he was able to hear her and understand what she was saying to him.

***

Tom got the call from Mrs. Pierce and felt sick to his stomach. Not for one second did he think of not going, despite his protestations at Christmas time. He felt deep in his being that it was serious this time.

He felt the panic rise within himself as he travelled by taxi to the airport to catch his flight.

His mind was emptied of all the legal wranglings beween Gilbrade and Kennedy Architects. It was filled only with thoughts of his father. He felt deep down that Danny's life was coming to an end. He felt lucky to have had Danny in his life. Danny may have wanted to come across as a simple farmer but he was much more than that. He was the wisest, kindest man Tom knew.

When Tom had trouble figuring the right thing to do about something, he would call Danny. Danny would normally equate whatever situation it was to something on the farm and come up with the sanest answer that Tom had ever heard. He had a great knack, a gift really, to see the sense in every situation.

◦◦◦

Tom rented a car at Cork airport and drove straight to the hospital. He went to the reception desk to find out where Danny was.

"Your father is in Intensive Care," the man on the desk informed him. He told him to take the lift to the third floor and gave directions to the ICU.

When Tom got there he was surprised to see Maud. He wondered if she had stayed at the hosptital for the whole day. He was struck by how beautiful she was sitting there, holding his father's wrinkled old hand.

"Hi," he said.

"Oh, Tom. Hi." Turning to Danny, she said, "Tom's here now, Danny. I'll leave you two alone. I'll come back and see you tomorrow."

She wasn't sure if she imagined it but she thought she felt him give her hand another squeeze. She hoped it was because he knew Tom had come.

"He's weak but he seems to understand what I'm saying to him. The doctors won't tell me anything naturally, because I'm not family."

"Thank you. Thanks for finding him and for staying with him. It means a lot to him, I'm sure. And to me. I'll contact you to let you know how he's doing."

"Yes, please do." Maud watched as he put her mobile number into his phone. "Goodnight then."

Tom put his hand on her arm as she passed him by. She felt an electric shock pass between them and he must have felt it too. He looked deep into her eyes and she thought he was going to kiss her again but of course that wouldn't be appropriate with Danny right there fighting for his life.

"See you, Maud, and thanks again. For everything."

# Chapter Thirty

Kate got a call from Justine Byrne two days later. She told the magazine editor about her new venture and Justine seemed suitably impressed by what she was doing. Kate emailed her photographs of some of her creations and Justine was blown away. She pencilled Kate in for a magazine spread three weeks from then. In the meantime an interview would have to take place and a photo shoot with Kate and her creations.

The day of the photo shoot arrived and Kate was up to ninety. She pulled everything out of her wardrobe and discarded every item she had. She had not been shopping in ages and it showed in the pathetic choice of clothes in her wardrobe.

Justine had said that they would take some photos in the bakery and she should wear her kitchen whites with the pink OTT Cakes logo so at least that part was sorted. But what would she wear for the other shots? She decided she had to go shopping so rushed in to the Powerscourt Centre where some young Irish designers were based.

She walked into Zara Roberts Design Shop and knew it was the place for her.

Zara took a huge interest in Kate and especially relished the idea that a gorgeous creature like her would be spread over pages of a glossy magazine wearing one of her own creations. The two women set about choosing the perfect look for the shoot.

After much trying on, Kate chose a tight-fitting 1940's style off-the-shoulder red velvet fitted dress. Not only did it have the same name as a type of cake but it made her look like one of the Hollywood movie stars of that era. The neckline plunged a bit lower than she would normally wear but she was assured by the designer that it wasn't indecent and showed just enough to attract the male readers but not enough to alienate the female ones.

Kate wasn't a stick insect and had never wanted to be. How could she be a stick insect and work with cake anyway? It just wouldn't be real. She was perfectly proportioned, with generous boobs and a small waist. She wasn't unaware of the glances she got when she was done up. She was certain that this dress would get her noticed in a very good way indeed.

Next stop was her hair. She called into Pzazz, which was "the place" to get your tresses tended to in the city. She tried to get an appointment. The guy on the reception desk looked at her with an expression that was a cross between pity and exasperation. He explained, very slowly and clearly, that if you wanted a Pzazz do, then you had to book r-e-a-l-l-y far in advance. She was about to turn on her heels and leave but stayed at the reception desk. She needed to be Pzazzed. She was about to be photographed for a major newspaper. She had the hottest dress that cost a small fortune. She wasn't going to let herself or the dress down by doing her hair at home herself.

The guy looked at her puzzled, wondering why she wasn't skedaddling. Maybe she had a hearing impairment, he thought.

"I'm sorry but I have a photo shoot this afternoon. For *Star Magazine*. I really need an appointment. I got this fabulous dress in Zara Roberts and I need fabulous hair to match it." She opened the bag and showed the hairdresser the wonderful red fabric.

"*Star Magazine*. Well, why didn't you say? I was just going to pop out for my break but I'll stay and give you a fab do. Come on over to the couch. We'll have a chat and decide what's gonna look best on you."

Kate couldn't believe her ears. There was a god after all. "The thing is, I haven't got a lot of time. I left it till the last minute because I was so busy and now ..." With that she burst into tears. Things had been so manic in the bakery that she hadn't allowed enough hours to prepare for the shoot.

"Ah, sweet cheeks, don't cry! We'll have you looking fabulous in no time. I'm thinkin' soft waves. You don't need a colour or anything so it won't take long, I promise," said her new best friend, trying to calm her down.

"Thank you. I'm sorry. I'm not normally like this but this is really important. Super-important, in fact."

True to his word the stylist did an amazing job while she told him about the bakery and shop and her hopes for the future. Her auburn waves shone like never before and would look wonderful with the red dress.

"Thank you so much. I'm delighted with it," she said, handing him a generous tip.

He gave her his details so that he could be credited in the magazine.

"Don't forget me when you hit the big time, love," he said as she stepped out onto the street.

# Chapter Thirty-One

Kate cordoned off part of the bakery for the photoshoot. It wasn't ideal in the middle of a busy day but the exposure she got from the magazine article would be worth it. She heard Ingrid shout that the photographer had arrived from the front of the busy shop.

"Hey. I'm Jack. Justine in the *Star* told you I'd be coming."

Kate shook hands with Jack and could not help notice how cute he was. Cute in a rugged handsome sort of way.

"Hi, I'm Kate. And I'm very nervous," she said by way of introduction.

"There's no need to be nervous. Just relax and smile and do everything I tell you to do."

Kate laughed when she realised that he was joking, trying to steady her nerves.

Luckily for her new hairdo, Jack did the non-bakery shots first.

He was really good-looking and he obviously thought she was too. He kept saying things like "stunning", "amazing", "gorgeous" and "fabulous". Maybe he said that to all the girls, Kate thought.

He took shots as she sat in the empty part of the coffee shop. She posed eating cake, sipping coffee. Looking sexily into the camera.

Dreamily looking into space. Kate normally wouldn't be comfortable with anybody telling her to lick icing off a fairy cake but Jack made it fun.

He was a professional after all and knew what he was doing. She relaxed and trusted his judgement and they had a great few hours together. She was pictured with several of her cake creations but Jack explained that they probably wouldn't all make it into the magazine.

He finished off by taking shots of the bakers hard at it in the shop. He somehow made it look like Candyland, with puffs of icing sugar and lots of pink fondant in the shots. He assured Kate that all the shots were great and that the only trouble would be picking which ones to include in the magazine spread.

She had really enjoyed the afternoon and was sorry to see him leave the shop. She had just turned to go back to the bakery when the bell sounded. She swung around to see Jack coming back in.

"Did you forget something?" she said, looking around for a discarded lens or camera bag.

"I forgot to ask you to go for a drink with me," he blurted out, sounding more nervous than the sentence suggested.

"Oh. Well. I, eh ..." Kate was blabbering.

"It's OK. It was a long shot. Sorry, I should have kept it professional," he said, looking embarrassed.

"*No*," she said in a louder voice than she actually intended. "That would be lovely. I'd love to. I was just trying to think when I'd have time to meet. You see, I work such long hours. But, feck it, I deserve a few hours off. I'll make an exception for you."

"Great," he said, looking relieved. "I have your number. I'll give you a call and we can go out whenever suits you. I can rearrange stuff. I will definitely rearrange anything to make sure I'm free when you are."

"OK. I'll talk to you tomorrow so. I'll have a look at my roster and find a gap."

"OK, great. Bye then. Till we meet again."

"Yeah, bye. *Au revoir.*" Oh God, what was she saying? Shut up. And she gave him a little wave as he went out the door.

She really needed to start having some fun as her life had become all work and no play whatsoever, making for a very dull Kate. She was leaning her head on her cupped hands, dreaming about the handsome photographer, when her phone rang.

It was Jack.

"I'm sorry, I know I should have tried to be cool and waited a few days before I called you but I really want to see you tonight. Are you free for dinner by any chance?"

"*Em.* Sure. Yes, why not? I've mountains of paperwork to do but I need to eat as well." She was surprised at how delighted she was to hear from him.

"Will I pick you up? Oh hell, I don't know where you live."

They arranged to meet in a little pub off Grafton Street because he had suggested a restaurant near there.

She buzzed around the coffee shop for the remainder of the day until it was time for her to leave. She was glad that her new hairdo would get another outing.

⇝⇝ ⇜⇜

Jack was already there when she got to the pub. He jumped up when she came in. He seemed nervous and Kate thought it was incredibly sweet.

"You look amazing," he said to her as she took off her coat and sat down.

"Thank you but I'm exactly as I was during the shoot," she replied.

"I just needed to tell you again. In case you thought I was only saying it in a professional capacity."

"You don't look too shabby yourself," she said, admiring his shirt that matched his grey-blue eyes.

"Look, we're both rides," he said, lightening the moment.

"That's more like it!" She laughed and watched his behind as he went to the bar to get her a drink.

He was funny and charming and incredibly good-looking. He was wearing jeans, a shirt and a leather jacket and he looked considerably underdressed for her designer outfit. He didn't seem bothered though and neither was she. She didn't care what someone was wearing as long as they were comfortable in their own skin. And Jack seemed to be.

He sat with his long legs stretched out in front of him and his arm draped over the back of the seat. She imagined he would be comfortable anywhere with his easy-going nature and his good looks. She had barely noticed the time going by when he indicated that it was time to go to the restaurant.

The dining room was packed and there was a buzzy atmosphere. It was one of Dublin's oldest restaurants and some might think a bit fuddy-duddy. Kate remembered wining and dining a few clients there in her corporate days. The maitre d' and Jack were on first-name terms and they were shown to a quiet booth towards the back of the room.

Jack asked Kate to choose the wine and she picked a Spanish Rioja. She took a sip of the wine poured by the waiter and declared it utterly drinkable. They both ordered monkfish tails and talked so much their food was cold by the time they ate it.

Kate normally loved her grub but she couldn't give a damn about the deliciously pan-fried monkfish. She only wanted to listen to Jack talk. He was gas. And incredibly interesting. He didn't only do photography. He was a filmmaker who had worked in the UK and in the US.

Jack too wanted to know everything about Kate. He asked why she left Dublin for the sticks of West Cork.

She told him all about how she ended up back in Inchahowen.

"You must have really loved your dad. To give everything up and go home to care for him," Jack said.

"*Eh,* let's say I did it out of a sense of duty rather than love."

"Oh, OK."

"I hope that doesn't sound ... *em* ... No, I ..."

"It's fine. You don't have to justify your decisions. The bit I know of you, I'm sure you did the right thing for the right reasons."

"*Hmm.* Anyway, let's talk about you. Your life is way more interesting than mine. Why did you leave New York?"

"I just missed the craic," he said simply. "The Yanks take themselves far too seriously. You couldn't go for a pint with someone without them working some angle. Everybody's on the make. Don't get me wrong, I'm as ambitious as the next guy but I don't want to sacrifice my whole life for my work."

"Ah, the elusive work-life balance."

"Ah yes. Well, when I got offered a job with the BBC, I thought I just might get the balance there. But London was crazier than New York. I was working nearly eighty hours a week every week. I did it for five years. All I did was work and sleep. Then I got a shout from an old mate here. He asked me to come back and make a movie with him. It got a newcomers award in Montreal and at the Schull Film Festival. I'm very big in County Cork."

"You're literally all anybody talks about in Inchahowen," she said, laughing. She watched him as he laughed heartily at himself. He was really damn handsome, she thought. And it wasn't the Rioja talking.

They both raised a toast to being big in Inchahowen and cracked up laughing again.

"Are you glad you stayed? In Ireland?" she asked.

She wondered if he would get up and go again and was already feeling she would miss him like crazy if he did.

"I met you, didn't I?"

She felt herself blush. She hoped the lights in the restaurant were dim enough so he wouldn't notice. She was giddy at the thought of him liking her as much as she liked him.

# Chapter Thirty-Two

The article on OTT cakes appeared on the front page of *Star Magazine* and when Kate saw it online she sank under the duvet and pulled it over her head. She thought she might never get up again. The article's headline read: "WE ARE GOING TO NEED CONSIDERABLY BIGGER CAKES" and showed a picture of Kate holding a cupcake in each hand strategically placed in front of each breast, just like in the movie *Calendar Girls*.

She had to admit that she looked fantastic in the photographs and once again thanked her lucky stars that she got Pzazzed that day. But was it the image she wanted to portray? She pulled herself out from under the duvet again and read the rest of the article. Justine had done a great piece on her and the rest of the photographs showed off her cakes and the bakery in a really cool light. Her phone was pinging with notifications. She didn't dare look at what people were saying. But when she saw her friend Maeve calling her, she picked up straight away..

"Well, well, well. When you said food porn, I couldn't have imagined such an incredible image," her friend said, laughing.

"Yeah, I don't know whether to laugh or cry. The rest of the article is actually really good and obviously I'm delighted with the publicity, but do you think it's too much?" she asked, unsure herself how this would be interpreted by the wider world.

"There's no such thing as too much when it comes to publicity. I think that Justine Byrne is your new best friend. You will bring that lady to lunch and you will thank her every day from the bottom of your heart for filling up your order book and making you a huge, and I mean *huge*, success. Seriously, Kate, the piece and the photographs are amazing. *Star Magazine* has a readership of a million people give or take a few thousand. I hope you're ready because you and OTT Cakes are going to be the talk of the town."

Kate had no doubt she was ready. She had planned everything with her usual precision and had been mentally working towards this place since she first started.

Her phone rang again and this time it was Jack.

"Are you still talking to me?" he said sheepishly.

"I was touch and go there for a while, but I suppose I am. The photographs look wonderful. Even 'that' one. I don't even remember posing like that."

"You don't see what I can see on the other side of the lens. It's the magic of photography. Your friend Justine did a great job. I've been thinking – we should make a tape."

"Haha! Don't you think that would be a bit risky? What if it fell into the wrong hands?"

"Not that kind of tape, you dirty thing! I mean a tape of you baking your cakes. Like a demo, you know. We could send them to the television networks. I think they would love you. You have star quality and those pictures prove it."

"Oh God, Jack, I don't know. Do you really think I could pull that kind of thing off?."

"I'm sure you could. I've photographed models and all sorts of famous people but you, my dear, are the real deal. You give off a 'I'm confident in my ability so everyone else can fuck right off' vibe. Not many people can achieve that level of confidence without seeming arrogant or mean. You could be huge."

Kate fell silent for a few moments. She was getting what she wanted. She wanted success but she wanted to be able to control it. Her head was all over the place. Then she said, "Do you want to come over and test their theory?"

"What theory?" he asked, puzzled.

"To see if we will need bigger cakes?"

"I'm on the way."

⇒⟫ ⟪⇐

Kate could not have anticipated the reaction to the article. When she got to work the following day her phone and her wonderful old door bell never stopped. The orders flowed in and she was glad that she had put the resources in place before the newspaper article came out. She was slammed with orders but wasn't fazed as she had the people and the equipment to meet all of them.

Orders weren't the only phone calls she was getting. She answered the phone in the shop to some strange individuals who were obviously more interested in the raunchy image that was portrayed of her. At one stage she had to tell a creepy guy who wanted to go out with her that she was a lesbian. It probably turned him on more, she thought as she hung up the phone.

But Kate didn't care. Today was one of the best days of her life.

⇝⇝ ⇜⇜

Jack had set up the filming for the weekend and he and Kate got down to the business of making the demo. He reckoned that they had to strike while the iron was hot and while Kate herself was hot news. It took them hours to get ten minutes of footage and Kate was beginning to get cranky with him for being so pernickety.

"We have to get this right. This is important so if I am being, *em*, pernickety, then excuse me. I want this to be perfect. Now if you don't mind, turn on that charm of yours and start looking like you're not being tortured to death."

Kate wondered if this filming was a big mistake. But something told her to just do it. She took Jack's direction and tried to act as naturally as she could. Even when he directed her to lick cake batter suggestively off a wooden spoon. They ended up in fits of laughter by the end of it.

Jack called to her apartment later that day with the finished edited version of what they would send out into the land of television producers and executives. She had to watch from behind her fingers, at first unable to associate the sexy voluptuous cakemaker with herself. Where did this woman come from? She was a million miles from the teenager trying to study in the chaos that was her childhood home with her alcoholic father and lazy sisters. But whoever she was, wherever she came from, Kate liked her. She came across as confident, sexy and funny. She prayed that RTÉ or the BBC or any other TV network would like her too.

"Well?" was all Jack said.

"It's fantastic. You are a very, very talented director to make me look that good," she said and leaned over to kiss him.

"It's all you, babe. You're going to be a huge star."

# Chapter Thirty-Three

There were lights coming up the driveway to Maud's house and she knew it was him. She opened the door to see him closing the driver's door of his rental car.

"Do you have any of that whiskey left?" he asked her as if he showed up at her house every day.

"Sure. I think I can rustle up a glass. Come on in," she said as if it was the most natural thing in the world to be inviting Tom Kennedy into her home. "What's the news on your dad?"

"He's comfortable. The doctors keep telling me that he's not out of the woods yet and I get the feeling they're trying to prepare me for the worst."

"Have you been with him all this time?"

"Yeah, I slept in a chair in his room last night. I'm a bit old for sleeping rough though. I could really do with sleeping in a bed tonight." He looked at Maud and saw that his comment made her uncomfortable. "*Eh*, I mean I booked into a hotel in Cork for the night."

"This is a bit of a detour then," she said, wondering why he would drive fifty miles out of his way when his hotel was in Cork city.

"I hope you don't mind me coming here. You've been so kind to my dad. I just wanted to give you an update on his condition. In person."

"You could have called or texted. It would have saved you a hell of a trip." But she was very glad he didn't. She couldn't help hope that the reason he was there was to pick up where he left off the last time. She poured two shots of whiskey and added ice as she had on Christmas Eve. She handed one to him. He took it and sat on the couch as he had done the last time he was there. They took in the moon's reflection on the inky black sea.

"I've thought about this view a lot lately," he said, after taking a large gulp of whiskey.

She wondered if he thought about her when he thought about the view but steered the conversation to safer territory.

"How are things going in London? You're working on a pharmaceutical plant?" She remembered he had mentioned it the last time he was here.

"You remembered? Yeah, we're still doing it. It will be a long-drawn-out project, probably taking up most of this year." He didn't want to tell her that he was after screwing up the future of his company.

The last thing he wanted to think about was the shitshow waiting at home for him in London. He wanted to talk about her. Find out everything he could about her.

"How come you're living here? I don't mean this house. This is beautiful. But why Inchahowen? Don't you find it a bit ..."

"What? Depressing? Quiet? Lonely? Remote? I have been asked all this by my parents. Well, my mom really. My dad's family are from here so I think on a certain level he understands what I see in this place."

"OK, well, what *do* you see in it?"

"It's hard to explain. It's like there are invisible chains keeping me here. Not chains even. Thread maybe is a better word. I love the ocean. Every day I get up and look out my window. It fills my soul with something that I know I won't get living in a city. I have thought about going home and buying a plot near the ocean. Maybe on Cape Cod and building a house there."

"It would make sense. At least you'd be near to your family."

"I came here to get away from my family in the first place. Or to be more precise, I came here to get them away from me."

"I don't understand," he said.

"My husband was killed in a plane crash."

"Jesus. I'm sorry."

"Thanks. It was ten years ago. It was horrendous but I was kinda getting over it. Then my brother was killed by a drunk driver one Christmas after he dropped me off at my apartment."

Tom wanted to reach for her, take her in his arms and take away her pain.

"I couldn't get away from everyone fast enough. I sold my business, leased my apartment, upped sticks and left."

"Jesus, I'm sorry about all of that loss. That's a lot of grief to live with. I'm not sure I could handle it. Do you ever get over it?"

Maud thought about Patrick appearing in her kitchen or in her mind the other night and decided not to share the experience with Tom. He'd definitely think the isolation had got to her. And maybe he'd be right.

"Yeah. I think I am getting there. When Ted died I was just heartbroken for all the years we wouldn't have together. I, well, we, wanted kids and I felt robbed of the chance to have our family. But when my brother Patrick was killed I blamed myself. If I had stayed the night in my mom and dad's house like they wanted me to, then Patrick would never have met that driver. But I think I'm at the point of forgiving myself now. Or, more importantly, I'm at the point of not feeling it was my fault." She was sorry she had told him any of this. It sounded really depressing when she put it out there.

She was sitting with her legs tucked up under her and her arm stretched out along the top of the couch. He, at the other end, put out his hand to touch her arm. She felt the electricity jolt her body when his fingers touched her. She wasn't sure if he had touched her by accident but he didn't take his hand away. Why were they playing games? Why not kiss her already?

"And you haven't met anybody since? That I don't understand. You're very beautiful," he said, moving towards her and looking deep into her eyes.

Maud could think of nothing but wanting his mouth on hers. "There isn't exactly a large pool of men to choose from around here. The good ones moved away," she said.

He moved closer into her space and at last kissed her on the lips.

"I'd like to see what you've done with the upstairs," he said. "Purely for architectural reasons."

"Of course," she said, smiling, and led him to her bedroom.

She had lain in her bed many nights since she first met him and imagined them making love with the candles flickering in the night air. Tom completely ignored the room's proportions or any architectural merit the space might have and concentrated fully on her.

His gentleness took her breath away and she could not get enough of his beautiful face and mouth. When his mouth started to travel down her body, she thought she would explode with happiness. He opened her shirt and bra and kissed her nipples which were already hard and peaked.

"You're beautiful," he muttered between kisses and she moaned in response.

She helped him take off his shirt and she admired his muscular chest and arms. They were both naked without a thought in the world for Danny or architecture or dead loved ones. There was only them.

# Chapter Thirty-Four

Tom awoke but closed his eyes again, holding her in his arms. He had almost forgotten how good it felt to hold a woman close. Valerie had made it clear to him for years that his advances were not welcome. After Molly was born she rejected his attempts to arouse her until he finally got the message loud and clear. She had given him what he wanted, she had done her wifely duty and produced a child. It probably wasn't as cut and dried as that but any time Tom tried to push the issue with her she would call him a selfish prick who didn't care about her or Molly but only about his "needs".

This was miles from the truth and he only wanted what anybody would want. He wanted to have a healthy sex life with his wife. He wanted to feel wanted and desired by the person he was married to

Sometimes she would give in to him and allow him have sex with her. He felt that she didn't fully participate in the act, rather she lay back and thought of England. Even though he didn't think he was being unreasonable, he started to question his ability in the bedroom and began to feel that there was something wrong with him. He wondered if another woman would find him attractive but these thoughts never led him to take any action to find out.

He was rational enough to know that even thinking about having an affair meant that his marriage was over. When he broached the subject and told his wife how he felt, Valerie looked like she couldn't care less. There was no talk about counselling or trying to mend things. Their marriage was finished.

⠠⠿⠇ ⠇⠿⠠

Tom thought he had better get up and go to see how Danny was. He gently nudged Maud and she raised her sleepy face to him. God, she was beautiful even with her tousled hair and remnants of last night's make-up still on.

"I really should get to the hospital," he said gently.

"Sure. I'll put on some coffee," she said, getting out of bed.

"Hold on. Not until you kiss me you don't!" He pulled her back to him.

She managed to extricate herself from his arms and put on her robe and went downstairs. Tom appeared a few minutes later as the coffee was brewed.

"Yes, it's very nice. Sympathetic to the old structure but given a modern twist."

"*Pardonez moi?*" she said, wondering if she missed something.

"The changes you made to the old cottage. That was why we went upstairs last night, remember?"

"Oh sure. Of course. I bet you made a big study of it alright. But where did you get the time?"

She laughed and he came over and wrapped her in his arms.

"I wish we could go back up there and have another look but I'd better get on the road. Thank you for your ... for everything. You'll never know how good it felt to hold you and to make love to you. I know it's a strange thing to say, but you feel like home."

"But I'm not your home – London is," she said wistfully.

"It's not far. It's a quick flight, that's all. I'm flying back this morning after I see Dad." He saw her disappointed face. "I'll be back this evening and call into the hospital again. Just one thing. Will I need to book a room at a hotel?"

"Don't you even think about going anywhere else but here," she said.

"I was hoping you'd say that."

He leaned in to kiss her. He could kiss her forever. Her mouth, her breasts, her thighs, her whole body in fact. It was perfect. She was perfect.

"I have to go. The sooner I go, the sooner I'll be back. See you tonight. I'll phone when my flight lands."

And with that he was gone.

Tom thought about Danny as he drove to the hospital. And about his meeting with his solicitors in London later that day. He couldn't wait to get his duties done and get back to Maud and her warm inviting place where he found perfect joy. She was funny and soulful and clever. He couldn't believe his luck in meeting her and he had to take his hat off to his father. He might be lying weak as water in a hospital bed, but he was still pulling the strings.

Maud watched Tom get into his car through the window in her living room. She wondered again how he could be so handsome. Danny was old so she couldn't see what he might have looked like as a young man. Rose must have been some looker, to have a son like that. She could feel every place his lips were – a shiver ran through her when she thought about their lovemaking. She thought she could die with happiness. She was helpless, it was hopeless, she was head over heels in love with Tom Kennedy.

# Chapter Thirty-Five

Tom arrived at the hospital at just past seven. Danny's condition hadn't changed. He hoped it a good sign but the doctor still warned him that Danny wasn't in the clear. There was a lot of damage done to his heart and operating was a challenge because of his age and his weak state. All they could do was wait and see.

Tom sat with Danny for a short while and held his hand. He told him that his matchmaking efforts had paid off and that he and Maud had finally got it together. There was no reaction from Danny. No gentle squeeze, no indication at all that he could hear his son or understand him.

Tom had to go to catch his flight and promised his father he would be back later in the day. He was not looking forward to meeting Doug and his team as they never seemed to have any good news for him about the case. Kennedy Architects was in negotiations to secure another contract. From Her Majesty's Government this time. Tom thought it would be a safer bet.

His bank confirmed that they were happy to take the deeds of the land as security for the loan of the money to fight Gilbrade. The bank had made contact with several valuers in Cork and Dublin to confirm that the land was worth what Tom said it was. At least he could stop worrying about the company's cashflow and paying his legal team. Now he only had to worry that he might lose everything including his inheritance. There were so many balls in the air that he felt like a circus act. If he dropped any one of them it would be curtains for him and for all the people who worked for him.

Looking at his father, pale and frail in the bed, his heart broke a little bit. It seemed obvious to Tom that Danny was leaving this life slowly but surely. Danny's colour wasn't good the night before, but he was waxy-looking now. Thinking about gambling with everything Danny had worked for brought more despair. He had to win the case. There was no two ways about it. He wouldn't be able to live with himself if he failed. Doug had to make sure they won.

The only good thing to have happened in his life recently was meeting Maud. And he had Danny to thank for that as well. Maud with her gorgeous lips and blue eyes. Her long limbs which were wrapped around him for most of the night. He wished that he could spend a week in her bed, making love and laughing but the gods were conspiring against him in that department. He braced himself for what he was about to face when he got back to London.

⁓≫≫ ≪≪⁓

Maud floated on air all day. She couldn't wait to see Tom again later that evening. She would cook dinner for them. She didn't want to go out anywhere. She wanted him all to herself. She shivered at the thought of their lovemaking the previous night. The memory of things he did to her made her blush. She was convinced that the customers must know exactly what she was thinking about as the images were so loud and vivid in her mind.

Tom had texted her before he got on the plane. She looked at the text again and her knees almost buckled. God, that man! "**Hi, beautiful. Danny is the same. I'll call back to see him this pm. Can't wait to get my hands on you later on. Tx.**

She left Eva looking after the coffee shop and went into the butcher's shop in the middle of the village.

The butcher, Seamus, was an organic farmer as well as a butcher. Maud took an age to decide what to buy. In the end she chose two fillet steaks. Seamus informed her that the steaks came from a bullock called Mossie. He even showed Maud a photo of the animal on his phone. Maud wasn't sure she wanted that level of detail but the steaks looked so good she went ahead and bought them.

⤞⤞ ⤝⤝

She took her time getting showered and dressed. She wanted everything to be perfect. She put on jeans and a T-shirt. It was February but, thanks to its energy upgrade, the temperature in the house was balmy. She tried to choose a pair of shoes but then decided to go barefoot.

She went downstairs and set the table. She lit candles galore. The candles would be the only light in the room. She put flowers she bought earlier in a vase in the centre. Linen napkins and crystal wine glasses completed the look.

The room looked fabulous but suddenly a thought struck her and stopped her dead in her tracks. Could she trust this joy she felt? Would fate intervene and declare that she wasn't entitled to such happiness? Only when she saw his car lights did she start to relax. She opened the door to him and he took her in his arms.

He kissed her deeply and passionately, the gentleness of the previous night gone.

"Hey! How was Danny? How was London?" she asked, between mouthfuls of him.

"London was fine. But Danny – I feel like he's slipping away."

"No!"

"The doctors say he's stable. That he could be unconscious for weeks. I can see it, though. It's like there's less of him there every time I walk into the room."

Maud couldn't bear to think of Danny like that.

"Do you think you should go back to him tonight?"

"No. There'll probably be no change in the next twelve hours. Anyway, I want to be here with you." He pulled to him and kissed her again.

Maud felt her head spinning. She had barely eaten all day and suddenly felt like she'd faint if she didn't have something.

"I'm making dinner. You hungry?" she asked, pulling herself away from him.

"Actually, yeah, I'm starving. Wow, it smells wonderful!"

"It's just onions and mushrooms so far. I've got steaks. How do you like yours cooked?"

"Rare, please," he said.

"Will you open the wine?" she asked.

She put the steaks in the hot pan while Tom poured the wine. He handed her a glass and went to the window with his own. She left him alone with his thoughts as she turned the steaks and cooked them for three minutes on the other side while she made a salad and put it in the centre of the table. She put mushrooms and onions on each plate, placing the cooked steak on top. She put the pepper sauce which she had made into a jug and placed that on the table also.

"OK, you ready?" she asked.

"Can't wait," he said. "This looks amazing. Sorry I was no help to you at all. I was lost in thought. I'll do the cleaning-up after."

They sat at the table and ate the delicious steaks. Maud had cooked them perfectly. Pink in the middle, just the way he liked it. They drank the wine and Maud laughed at the pleasure he was taking out of the food.

He ate like he made love. He savoured every bite, rolled his eyes in ecstasy and groaned in pleasure with every bite of the juicy meat.

After the steaks were eaten and their plates were empty, they stayed at the table and talked. They each wanted to know so much more about the other.

Maud told Tom about the times they visited Inchahowen as children. Tom told her about the boys from Boston he met one summer and they came to the realisation that they were Maud's brothers.

"How come I never met you?" he asked.

"I used to go to Paris with my mom. The boys would come here with my dad for a few weeks before joining us in Paris. The boys preferred running wild around the countryside than having to sit quietly in their grandmother's living room. My dad felt the same way as the boys."

They talked about what their lives would be like if they had met each other all those years ago. Tom declared that Maud would probably be barefoot in the kitchen, as she was actually barefoot in the kitchen that night, and that they would have five children. All girls and all the image of their mother, tall and blonde.

Maud declared that it would in fact be Tom who was barefoot in the kitchen and that they would have all boys who were tall, dark and handsome like their father. They would adore her and wait on her hand and foot when she came in from a hard day's work.

"That'd work," said Tom. "I would stay at home all day and wait for you. I have been waiting for you all my life, in fact."

Maud felt exactly the same way. She felt as if they had known each other forever. Not the short time it actually was. Even Ted would approve, she thought. Ted was the benchmark upon which all others were measured. Tom measured up just fine.

He was a man's man but he also had a gentle, sensitive side. She wondered if her family would get the chance to meet him. Maybe they would to to Boston for a weekend. Hopefully Tom could get away from work. Her mind was running away with her. She had to stop herself. Normally when something good happened to her, something bad was just around the corner.

⤙⤙⤙ ⤙⤙⤙

Sometime in the middle of the night, Tom's phone rang. He jumped out of bed but couldn't find it. Maud almost laughed at how comical it was seeing him naked firing clothes around the room trying to find the source of the ringing, but the fact that somebody was calling him at four in the morning could not be for any good reason. The phone had stopped by the time he found it.

"*Shit*. It's the hospital," he said.

He dialled back the number and Maud heard him say that he would be right there.

"It's Danny. He's taken a turn for the worse. His breathing is weaker. They think I should be there."

"Do you want me to come with you?"

"No. I'll call you later and let you know what's going on. They're probably just being cautious. He's resilient if nothing else."

And with that he was gone. He had barely kissed her, he was in such a hurry to get out the door.

Poor Tom. Poor Danny. Maud had a sinking feeling that it was the end for Danny. She wished she had gone with him. But he was adamant. Maybe he wanted to be alone with his father to see him cross over to wherever good souls go.

She could still smell Tom in the room and she rolled over to "his" side of the bed and tried to fall back to sleep.

# Chapter Thirty-Six

The phone woke Maud again a few hours later. It was Tom to tell her that Danny had passed away. He was with him at the end and she was glad for that. She wouldn't forgive herself if Tom was in bed with her while Danny took his last breath.

Maud was saddened by the news. Danny was her first proper friend in Inchahowen and she would miss him. He was the first neighbour to call and welcome her. He made her feel like she was a part of the small community, for which she would be forever grateful to him.

Maud wasn't sure whether to expect Tom back that day. He would have a lot to do making all the necessary funeral arrangements. She couldn't decide whether to call him to see if he wanted her to go to the hospital. In the end she decided to leave it up to him to contact her if he needed anything. She was being selfish. She wanted him near her, touching her, telling her she was part of his future. Instead he had the terrible task of dealing with his father's death.

Maud decided that she would be better off at work. News had reached Inchahowen already that Danny had died. Nobody talked about anything else as they ordered their coffees and pastries. Maud felt like a real part of everything as she shared her own anecdotes and stories about her lovely neighbour.

⤛⤜

Tom phoned later that day to say that he was flying back to London and would be back in two days. He told her that the funeral would not take place until then. He had arranged everything with the undertakers and Danny's body would stay in the funeral home until Tom brought him home to wake him in the house for the last time.

"How are you? Are you OK?" she asked him tenderly.

"I am. He wasn't going to live forever and I suppose I was expecting this day to come. I'm glad I was with him at the end. I was holding his hand and I think he knew that I was there. I think he knew I loved him and how grateful I was for everything he did for me. I didn't say it to him enough. He used to hate it when I tried to show him any affection. It was just his generation, I guess. I kissed his lips before I left him and they were cold. I mean already cold. Life is so fucking fragile. One minute you're a living, breathing human being and the next you're cold as a stone."

Maud thought she heard his voice catch in his throat which almost set her off crying.

"Danny adored you and you made him so proud. You two didn't need to say it every day. You both just knew," she said soothingly.

"I hope you're right. Look, Maud, I've got to go. I'll call you before the funeral."

And with that, he was gone. Again.

She hadn't thought this was the way things would be with them. She didn't think that a place would exist where doubt could flourish. She was probably imagining it. They had a bond, a connection. Anyway people acted oddly around death. She knew that first hand. She would let him grieve in whatever way he needed to.

# Chapter Thirty-Seven

Tom left his father in the hands of the undertakers who arrived at the hospital from Inchahowen an hour after he phoned them. They assured him that they would take care of Danny's remains until Tom returned to Cork.

Tom cursed the fact that he had a meeting with his legal team. He could have cancelled but it was too important and there was way too much at stake. Danny was gone. But his fight with Gilbrade was about to start. *Round 1.*

In the taxi to his office from the airport he thought again about using Danny's money for that fight. What if he lost his legal battle? What if Danny's life's work was to go into the coffers of a greedy fucking pharmaceutical company and the legal team defending them?

"You have to fucking make sure we win, Da."

"Sorry, mate?" the taxi driver said.

Tom had no idea he had spoken out loud. He was all over the place. But what did he expect? His father had died a few hours ago. His anchor in the world. The person who loved him without condition.

"Sorry. Nothing."

Doug was in his office when Tom walked in.

"I'd hoped to have better news for you. We gave them a figure we'd settle for, but Gilbrade are intent on going the whole nine yards with this."

Tom put his head in his hands. He did hold out a tiny bit of hope that they would settle but his instinct told him that was never going to happen. Not with a company like Gilbrade. They were the schoolyard bully. They'd kick the shite out of you and steal your lunch money while they were at it.

He was tired and he was emotional. His resolve was coming and going in waves. Part of him wanted to tell Doug to forget the whole thing. But he had to go after the bastards. Danny was a fierce man for fighting the good fight. He was very principled and Tom had inherited the trait from him.

"Are you alright?" Doug asked.

"My father died early this morning."

"What? You're ... Oh mate, I'm sorry. You should have said and we could have rescheduled."

"No. No rescheduling. I want to do this and I don't want any delays. The sooner it gets started, the better. I might not have the resolve to do it at a later date."

"Right. Well, I'm sorry to ask, but you will have to transfer some funds into my client account. I know the money is from the land ..."

"Yes, of course. It's my land. My fight," said Tom.

It was the first time he had used the words "my land" and it felt like more than just words. Some of the land belonged to generations of Kennedys before his father and some of it was bought by his father purely for him. *Jesus, Dad, what if I lose it all? How will I live with myself?* He knew his father was only really entrusting the land to him and laying down a challenge of doing something with it that would benefit the local community in Inchahowen. *No pressure then, Tom.*

⤐⤐⤐ ⫷⫷⫷

The next stop Tom made was to the house in Notting Hill. He wanted to tell Molly in person that her grandfather was dead. Knowing Valerie, she would just tell her the news, giving it the same billing as what was for dinner. Normally Valerie made him stand at the door for ages before letting him in, making him feel like he never lived there. Today, she let him in straight away. She offered him a drink when they got to the kitchen.

He was discombobulated by her out-of-character behaviour but he had no time to analyse it.

"Danny died. This morning. Massive heart attack."

"I heard. Joanna told me. Oh Tom. I'm sorry, I know how much you loved him!" Valerie was   showing concern that Tom never knew she felt. "Why are you not still in Ireland?"

"I was. When he died. I had to come back for … just some work stuff needed sorting. I'm going back as soon as …" he said, unable to continue.

The shock of Danny's death hit him then. He started to cry. He tried to leave the room so that Valerie wouldn't witness his blubbering. She normally hated public displays of any type of emotion. She especially hated anyone showing weakness.

But to his enormous surprise and shock, she went to him and held him as he sobbed. She comforted him and told him to let it all out. She allowed him to lean on her. Somebody really ought to bring the real Valerie back, he thought. It felt wrong. All wrong. He pulled himself together and pulled out of her embrace.

"Is Molly here? I want to tell her."

"She's watching TV. We'll tell her together, shall we?"

Tom wondered again about the real Valerie's whereabouts, and who this impostor was.

"*Em*, OK," he said.

They went to the lounge and found Molly watching something that Tom thought was thoroughly unsuitable viewing for a six-year-old child. Now wasn't the time for any argey-bargey with Valerie though so he let it go.

They sat their daughter down and told her the sad news. Tom was touched that she ran to him and hugged him. She didn't see Danny very often but she was fond of him nonetheless.

"What will happen to the calves and the lambs, Daddy? Will they die too?" she asked in her sweet little innocent voice.

"No, darling. Another farmer will mind them. You'll still be able to visit any time you want." Then Tom realised that if the court case went against them, there would be no visiting Inchahowen for them.

"That's good. Granddad showed me how to give the lambs milk from the bottles. I can help you, Daddy. I'm watching my programme now though."

Tom and Valerie left Molly watching what looked terribly like an adult chat show.

"It's fine," Valerie said as they were leaving the lounge, noticing Tom's unease about Molly's choice of programme.

"Should she not be watching *Paw Patrol* or something?"

"She prefers Dr. Phil to Chase or Marshall. What can I say?"

Back in the kitchen Valerie poured a drink for him. Her thoughtfulness was discomfiting.

"When is the funeral?" she asked, handing him the tumbler.

"The day after tomorrow. It's not like here. We bury our dead quickly in Ireland." He took a drink and stared into the glass. "I want to take Molly with me."

"Of course. Danny was her grandfather. We'll all go."

"I don't expect you to ..."

"Nonsense. He was my father-in- law after all. And Tom, please don't refer to me as your ex-wife while we're there. Molly doesn't like it."

*Newsflash. You are my ex-wife*, he was about to say but stopped himself.

He heard himself agree to her request. He'd had enough drama for one day.

"Do you want to stay tonight?" Valerie asked. "In the spare room if you prefer?"

In the spare room if he preferred? Of course he bloody preferred. In fact he didn't want to stay there at all. He wanted to be with Maud. He craved the comfort of her. Her kindness which was authentic and unlike whatever was going on with his ex.

"No. I'll go to my flat. I'll book the flights this evening and text you on the times later. I'll pick you both up in a taxi in the morning."

"We'll be ready."

# Chapter Thirty-Eight

Tom was sure that Valerie's onset of concern for his welfare would have dissipated before the flight to Ireland but it hadn't. She was a very different person to the angry, sarcastic woman he left a few months before. She encouraged Molly to sit with him and talk to him about her grandfather. Tom's emotions were all over the place as it was and Valerie's behaviour was starting to tip him over the edge.

The air hostess handed a colouring book and pencils to Molly and Tom watched as Valerie helped their daughter colour in a picture of an elephant and a circus tent. Even Molly seemed puzzled by her mother's sudden attention to her. She stole a few glances at Tom but he just smiled at her and with his eyes encouraged her to go with it.

Tom used the time to think about his father. He couldn't quite believe that he was never going to see him again. Never going to hear any of the old sayings or the old man's wise words. His father was the only person on the planet who loved him without condition. Tom's mind wandered to where his father might be now. With Rose? Danny and Rose back in each other's loving arms? No, he decided. He was nowhere. He was nothing now. Dust. *And unto dust thou shall retur*n.

When the plane landed in Cork, Tom watched as Valerie organised the hire car and took control of getting the three of them to West Cork. She even insisted on driving. He sat in the passenger seat, lost in his own thoughts while Valerie, uncharacteristically patient, negotiated the windy roads while answering Molly's many questions.

⤜⋙ ⋘⤏

The car pulled up outside Danny's house. Tom's house now. The funeral director was waiting for him. All their neighbours and friends were gathered outside in the cold, waiting to pay their respects.

"I'm sorry for your loss, Tom," Pádraig the undertaker said.

"Thanks, Paud. I appreciate all you've done, with me being in London."

"It's no bother, boy. We've laid him out in the parlour. Mrs. Pierce picked out a suit for him. He looks great. Like himself."

Tom smiled inwardly. *The dead man looks great. What a relief! Danny would be delighted to hear it.* But he knew what Paud meant. Some people die in horrific circumstances, and it took a lot of skill to get the deceased to resemble their live selves.

"Is anybody with him?"

"No. You'll be the first one. You'll want to see him by yourself, I'm sure."

Tom walked in through the kitchen door with Valerie and Molly in his wake. The room looked the same, smelled the very same. Except it wasn't. Nothing would be the same ever again. His mother and father who loved him to his very core were both now gone. He heard himself gasp and felt Valerie's hand on his back, gently nudging him in the direction of the front room.

"I'll stay here with Molly. I don't think we should ... she should ..."

"You're right," Tom said. "I'll go in alone."

The room smelled of furniture polish. Mrs. Pierce had been busy. His father was laid out in an mahogony casket with gold-coloured handles. Tom had stated to Paud that he wanted the most expensive coffin they had. As coffins went, it was very nice. His father deserved the very best. He noticed that the coffin matched the upright piano that his mother used to play. He ran his hands along the casket without looking at him. It took him a few moments before he was able to focus on the body lying inside.

Danny was holding a pair of rosary beads in his folded hands. Tom had a bit of trouble disentangling the beads from his father's cold dead grasp. He knew that Danny wouldn't oppose a Christian burial but there was no way he'd have wanted to be seen as a Holy Joe. He still had a healthy dose of disdain towards the Catholic church.

He looked at Danny and put his hand on his father's cheek. The cold startled him even though it was expected. He didn't look great, didn't look like himself. He looked like a corpse. He was waxy and he was dead. Danny's life was in his twinkly eyes. The eyes were closed and the twinkle was gone. He could harldly believe he'd never see it again.

The swell of pain rose from somewhere inside him and manifested in a noise that Tom wasn't sure had even come from him at all. Valerie came running into the room. She put her arms around him and stood like a tower of strength as Tom once again cried like a baby into her hair.

⟫⟫⟩ ⟨⟨⟨⟨

They opened the house to the waiting crowd who then milled around the place for what seemed like hours. The priest arrived at half past nine and said prayers over Danny's coffin. The rosaries sounded like chanting as those inside the house and those who had to stand outside due to the volume of the crowd answered the priest in unison. Once the prayers were over, some people took it as their cue to leave. Tom shook hundreds of hands and watched as Valerie graciously shook the same hands and accepted their condolences as if she was personally affected by the death of her father-in-law.

Most of Danny's old friends stayed on. There were bottles of whiskey, apple tarts and trays of sandwiches on every surface. The people of West Cork knew how to do death.

Tom was glad that he decided on having the wake. Bottles of whiskey were drunk and ham  and egg sandwiches were eaten. There were tears of laughter mixed with sadness as the people in Danny's life shared their experiences with each other.

Tom had seen Maud in the crowd at one stage. She was hanging back as if not to intrude. As if! She had been a great friend to his father. He suddenly felt bad for not contacting her since he'd left her house to return to London.

He sent her a quick text. **Hi. I'm sorry for not being in touch before now. Things have been crazy. I saw you this evening and I wanted to say hello but when I turned around you'd disappeared. I'll see you at the funeral tomorrow? x**

"Who are you texting?" Valerie asked.

Tom for the strangest reason felt he was betraying his ex-wife. "Nobody. Nothing. It's stuff – work," he lied.

"Forget about work for the next few days, Tom. You need to focus on yourself now. And your family."

Tom wondered what the fuck was going on in Valerie's head. Family? Surely she didn't mean him, Valerie and Molly? His phone beeped and interrupted his thoughts.

**Hi. I hope you're OK. That's a stupid thing to say – of course you're not OK. And yes, I'll see you tomorrow. Let me know if I can do anything.** X

# Chapter Thirty-Nine

As the last stragglers left the house in the early hours, Tom closed the back door. They were alone now. Well, alone apart from Danny in another room. He saw Valerie turn up her nose at the old fixtures and fittings in the house and asked for the umpteenth time since she started coming to Ireland why there wasn't a hotel nearby.

Tom was amused at her discomfort and glad to see that the real Valerie was lurking just under the surface after all. They had put Molly to bed hours before, in Tom's childhood room where she always stayed on their rare visits. She insisted that Ned, Danny's old dog, be allowed to sleep at the foot of her bed. Tom was too tired to argue so the hairy mutt and his beautiful little girl settled down to sleep for the night.

"Right. Time for bed, busy day tomorrow," he said.

He hadn't given any thought to the sleeping arrangements, but he was shocked to hear Valerie say that they would share the bed in the spare room.

"I'll sleep in Da's bed. You sleep in the spare room," he said.

"You can't sleep in a dead person's bed, Tom. That's too creepy," Valerie argued.

It had been a long day and Tom had drunk a few glasses of whiskey. Nor did he relish the idea of sleeping in Danny's bed. He used to believe in ghosts when he was a child and he didn't imagine he would get a wink of sleep. He found himself agreeing to sleep in spare room.

Tom watched as Valerie started to undress. He wondered if he wouldn't have been better off taking his chances with the ghosts. He punched his pillows and said goodnight to Valerie. He remembered there was a dip in the middle of the mattress as soon as Valerie got under the covers. He held on to the edge of the mattress for dear life. Despite his best efforts, they both ended up in the dip. Tom felt her hands on his chest and he was temporarily paralysed. His brain knew what was happening but it was like it was happening to somebody else entirely. Things got stranger when Valerie started to kiss him. Her lips were very different to Maud's and not familiar to him any more. He wanted to push her away but he didn't know how to reject her advances. He was so stunned and thrown. Then to his complete bewilderment, he wasn't even sure if he wanted to reject her.

"I'm sorry for the past, Tom. You know I've always loved you. You do, don't you? Look at what we have achieved together? We have Molly and our beautiful home. I was stupid, Tom. I was just so damned stupid." Her lips were on his again.

His mind was in turmoil and his emotions were not to be trusted.

"You don't want this, Val. You've developed some kind of misplaced empathy. My father has died but I'm OK. I'm going to be OK. I don't need you to …"

"*Shhh* …" she said, running her finger along his mouth

She was now completely naked and was sitting on top of him. He felt himself stiffen beneath her. He hadn't seen her naked breasts for a long time and he had to admit to himself that she was still stunningly beautiful. Her mouth was on his and he hungrily kissed her. He didn't wrestle with his conscience but instead wrestled with his ex-wife in the spare room in his dead father's house. He threw her off him onto her back and opened her legs wide. It had been a long time since they had wanton sex but he hadn't forgotten what turned her on. She liked him to take charge, to take what he wanted. She lifted herself to him and he exploded inside her. He heard her gasp and felt her spasms.

"I love you," she said.

He almost believed her but he didn't say it back. His brain was fogged up again. He got off her and lay back on his pillows, on his side of the bed. *Fuck.* Valerie had her hands on his chest, both of them wedged together in the middle of the bed. He remained silent, not at all sure what his next move should be.

He felt awful. How did he let that happen? Why did he not stop himself? Why did he not tell Valerie that he had met someone else, that it was over between them for good? He was in a weakened state and Valerie knew it. For whatever reason, she wanted to have sex with him. She wasn't normally a spontaneous person. Every action was thought out and premeditated. He pulled back the covers and started to get up.

"Where are you going?" Valerie asked.

"I'll sleep on the couch. I'm sorry. That shouldn't have happened. I'm not thinking straight."

"Lie back down, silly. You need to get some sleep. It will be a long day tomorrow."

Tom didn't argue. He didn't fancy sleeping on the hard sofa in the living room anyway. He did what he was told and soon heard Valerie snoring softly on her side of the bed.

While Valerie slept like a baby, Tom lay beside her, wide awake. He couldn't make sense of anything.

# Chapter Forty

Maud was caught up in the funeral and the collective grief shared by the villagers. She didn't open up on the day of the funeral as a mark of respect to one of the Inchahowen's oldest residents. She had an uneasy feeling about Tom. She hadn't expected to be up front in the church as chief mourner with him but she had only got one text from him and even that was just a vague "**How you doin'?**"

She would let him know that she was there for him when she saw him after the Mass. She walked into the church and looked for a free space. It was packed to the gills. A stranger scooched up and offered Maud a seat beside her. Maud mouthed her thanks and sat down gratefully.

There was now standing room only in the tiny church. Maud couldn't see Tom with the amount of people in attendance. The bells rang and the Mass started. The congregation prayed in unison and Maud could almost appreciate what people got out of going to church. The priest gave a eulogy and portrayed Danny as a great man who wanted nothing more than to work hard for his family and have Tom back in Inchahowen.

Everyone smiled and bent their heads knowing that it was exactly what Danny wanted. Most of them knew that Danny's wish would never come true. Tom would never come back to Inchahowen.

After the Mass was over, Tom and some men from the village carried Danny's coffin down the aisle of the church. Maud was so moved by the sight of the man she loved carrying the remains of his father, the last remains of his family, and the physical effort imprinted on his handsome face. He walked past and did not see her. She could see tears running down his face and it brought tears to her own eyes. She wanted to stand beside him and comfort him. She wanted to show him how much she loved him. Most of all, she wanted to bring light and joy back into his life.

People started to leave the church after the coffin and Maud noticed a beautiful woman with a little girl. It must be Valerie and Molly, she thought. She was shocked to realise that she hadn't expected them to be there. Molly was Danny's only grandchild. Of course she would be there. And obviously Valerie wanted to be there for her daughter.

Maud was struck by what a stunning woman Valerie was. Why had she never given her any thought before now? They must have made a truly amazing couple. She suddenly felt jealous. Outside the church people lined up to shake hands with Tom and Valerie. She could hear Tom thanking people for coming and introducing them to his wife and Molly. *His wife! Ex-wife surely? Oh Tom, please don't say that you lied to me!* She couldn't bring herself to face the two of them. She didn't want him to introduce her to his wife. She couldn't bear it.

"Hey, Maud, wait up!" someone called.

"*Kate!* Hi! I didn't expect to see you here," said Maud, relieved to see a friendly face.

"You'd be excommunicated if you missed a funeral in Inchahowen. I knew Emer and Grace wouldn't bother coming, so I drove down. Aren't you going to sympathise with Tom?"

"No. He has a lot of people around him right now. I'll catch up with him some other time."

"The ex-wife is a piece of work. She couldn't stand Danny. Made it obvious too, old wagon! She used to hold her nose when she was around him. Plenty of breeding but no manners," Kate said disgustedly.

"I don't know if the 'ex' part is accurate. He's introducing her as his wife," Maud said and almost burst into tears.

Kate could see that Maud was upset and mistakenly took it as being due to Danny's death.

"Come to the pub. We can raise a glass to Danny, the old divil," she said, grabbing Maud by the arm and leading her towards Seán's.

The pub was getting busy with the crowd from the funeral. The priest had announced from the altar that there would be soup and sandwiches and a free bar in Seán's after the burial and practically the whole locality were there. Maud spotted a free table right at the back of the pub. Kate told Maud to grab the table while she went to the bar and arrived back with two glasses.

"Is that whiskey? I'm not drinking that, Kate. It's only one o'clock in the day."

"It's a funeral. We do this. We bury whichever poor frigger happens to be dead and we get pissed. Look, don't argue. It's the rules." Kate took a sip of hers, making a face as the whiskey hit the back of her throat. "So you'll miss Danny?"

"Yes. I liked him a lot. We had a lot of fun times. I helped him deliver a calf on New Year's Eve."

"You? Delivered a calf? You're more the eat-the-calf variety."

"Yeah. I'm not exactly a country gal, more city slicker. Anyway we just shared this kind of special experience. I was in a bad place. My mom and dad had just gone back to Boston and I was feeling pretty sorry for myself. You know. I was facing into another year on my own *blah blah*. It was just a nice thing to happen."

"He was a special man, was Danny. He was also the greatest pain in the arse sometimes. His heart was in the right place though."

"He told me all about his wife that night. And Tom. He adored both of them," Maud said with tears in her eyes.

"*Aw*, Maud. Danny had a good life. He loved Rose and Tom. He loved Inchahowen and his animals. Especially Ned. You'll probably have to adopt him now, by the way."

"Look, Kate – it's not Danny I'm upset about. It's Tom."

"Tom? Sure he'll be grand. He's some big-shot architect in London. You can save your tears there, I'd say."

"I love him."

"Danny? Sure we all –"

"*Tom*. I love Tom."

Kate looked at Maud and knew she meant it. The pain of loving someone showed in her face. "Maud? What's going on?"

The noise in the pub died down suddenly. Maud and Kate looked up and saw that Tom, Valerie and Molly had just walked in. Maud felt crushed all over again. She couldn't bear to see them together like the picture-perfect family. Tom had Molly up in his arms and Valerie had her hand on Tom's back as if her hand was the only thing keeping him upright.

"What?" Kate said. "How come I didn't know about this? You better start talking."

Maud told Kate everything. From the first kiss the night she had cake batter on her face to their first kiss to his appearance in the pub that very minute.

"Jesus! What a prick! Parading Valerie into the pub right under your nose. I know he's a cousin of mine, but I'd like to give him a piece of my mind.

"He's your cousin? How come you're only giving me this bit of information now?"

"Keep up, Maud! I already told you Danny and my mother were first cousins. He's some sort of cousin. Like once removed. Or twice even. I told you everyone in Inchahowen is related. You and I are probably related too if we went back far enough. Anyway, that's not the point. The point is what are you going to do now? Are you going to talk to him?"

"What? No. Of course not."

With that Maud found herself being dragged by Kate towards the front door of the pub.

"Tom, I'm terrible sorry for your loss," Kate said, pushing past a group of people who were sympathising with him. She shook his hand. "And you must be Valerie." She shook her hand too.

"*Em*, yes. Thank you for your condolences. But he had a good life," Valerie said, as if she had the first clue about Danny's time on earth.

"Yes, indeed." Kate then pushed Maud almost up against Tom's chest.

"Hey," he said awkwardly.

"Hello. How are you?" Maud asked without looking directly at him.

"I'm ... Maud, I ..." Tom's sentence was cut off abruptly.

"Darling, Claire and Edgar are leaving," said Valerie, practically pushing Maud out of the way and putting her hand on Tom's shoulder. "Sorry but they're our friends. They came all the way from London this morning for the funeral. We really should say goodbye to them."

Maud watched Valerie manhandle the man she loved away and over to the couple who presumably were Claire and Edgar. Tom looked back over his shoulder at Maud but she looked away.

"I need to get out of here," she said to Kate.

"You are not going anywhere. Especially not back to that empty house to mope around and feel sorry for yourself. We are going to raise a glass to Danny and we are going to get as drunk as fucking lords!"

# Chapter Forty-One

Tom cursed Edgar and Claire for coming to the funeral. Had they not come or if their timing had been better, then he could have spoken to Maud. He could have explained or at least attempt to anyway, how everything had spiralled out of control. He could have told her that he and Valerie were not husband and wife, no matter how many times Valerie introduced herself as that.

He winced every time he heard her say it but he couldn't do anything about it. What could he do? Announce to the village that they were in fact divorced and that his ex-wife was having some kind of mental episode?

He wished he could have told Maud that he loved her and that she was the best thing that had happened to him. But he could hardly look her in the eye. He was ashamed for having succumbed to Valerie's advances. How had he been so stupid? He would come clean but today, the funeral, wasn't the time or the place.

It didn't escape his notice that she had looked hurt. He hadn't missed the look on her face when he treated her like an acquaintance instead of the woman he wanted to spend the rest of his life with. Falling in love with her was sudden and unexpected. He knew that but it made perfect sense to him. She made perfect sense in a senseless world.

Everything in his life was upside down. His father had just died. His ex-wife was pretending like they were still married and still meant something to each other. His business was hanging by a thread and he was gambling everything his father had worked for on saving it. How was he meant to think straight?

The only peace he had felt recently was when he was with Maud. She made everything clear in his mind. When he was with her, nothing else mattered. He didn't care about being a successful architect. If he had Maud he would be happy to live with her in Inchahowen and start all over again designing dormer bungalows or taking a job in a firm in the city and arriving home to her every night.

But here and now with everything going on, Valerie was taking ownership of him and he was allowing it. It broke his heart to see Molly so happy at having both her parents together. Christ, if he could just get through this day. If he could just see Danny off in the way he would have wanted with all his friends and the whole village telling stories about him and laughing and joking their sadness away.

⤞⤝

Tom flew back to London with Valerie and Molly that evening. It was past midnight when the taxi stopped outside the house in Notting Hill. Molly had slept on the plane and in the taxi from the airport. She was cranky by the time they got her inside.

"I want Daddy to tuck me in," she said,

"Darling, it's late. Mummy will tuck you in tonight. I'll see you tomorrow," Tom said.

"*Noooo!*" she wailed. "*I want you, Daddy!*"

"I'll do it," he said to Valerie and took his daughter by the hand and climbed the stairs to her bedroom.

"Are you still sad?" Molly asked as Tom pulled her pyjama top over her little head.

"I'm still a little bit sad, Moll. It's always a little bit sad when somebody you love dies."

"Is Granddad in heaven?"

Tom was taken aback by Molly's question. He and Valerie didn't talk about faith around their daughter. She attended a non-denominational school and they really hadn't given much thought to bringing Molly up in any religion at all.

"Em ... yes, I suppose he is. Would you like it if he was there?"

"Yes, I think I would. He'd live on a fluffy cloud and eat Philadelphia."

It took Tom a second or two to realise that Molly had taken her cues from the ad on TV for the cream cheese. Fucking hell, he thought. If her parents didn't get their act together and start filling in the blanks, God knows where she would get her information from. For tonight, Tom decided to leave Molly with the vision of her granddad on a fluffly cloud, eating cream cheese. He was way too tired to disabuse her of that notion just now.

Molly fell asleep almost as soon as her head hit the pillow. Tom stayed with her a few minutes to make sure she was out for the count. When he was certain that she was, he went back down to the kitchen which was in the basement of the three-storey house. Valerie handed him a glass of whiskey as soon as he walked in. She didn't drink whiskey as far as he knew, so the bottle must have been there since he was still living in the house.

"Thanks," he said.

"Are you OK? After today, I mean," she asked him.

"I'll be fine. It hit me when they laid him in the ground that I'll never see him again. I owe him so much, Val. He wanted me to ... Oh, forget it. It doesn't matter now." He really didn't want to go over this with Valerie. She wasn't given to wasting emotions over a dead person even if that dead person was his father. He wanted Maud. She would understand how he felt. She would know how to soothe him.

"Of course it matters. He thought the world of you. He wouldn't have wanted you to think you owed him anything. If you were in his place, you wouldn't want Molly to think that, just because you wanted the world for her, she owed you something in return."

"No, of course not." There was no point in having this conversation with her. She wouldn't understand the sacrifices that Danny made for him or the opportunities that he gave to him to get his education and how hard it was for Danny when Tom settled in London. Valerie was born with a silver spoon in her mouth. Struggle and challenge were not words in her vocabulary.

"Molly is so happy having both of us around," she said.

"*Hmm*," Tom said, continuing to sip his whiskey.

"You know we could make this a more permanent arrangement."

"What do you mean? A more permanent arrangement?"

"You and I. We could try again. You could move back ..."

"*Whoa!* No. I ... I mean, why would you even suggest such a thing?"

"The last few days have been different between us. Don't tell me you haven't felt it too, Tom."

"Of course the last few days have been different. My father is dead. You don't lose a parent every day. Jesus, Val. Surely you don't think ... *Jesus!*"

"What about in bed the other night? Don't say that you didn't enjoy it. Because I know you'd be lying. I certainly did."

"*Jesus Christ!* Before we split up you wouldn't even let me touch you. You acted like you were repulsed by me. What happened in Inchahowen was a mistake. It should never have happened."

"But we used to be great together. It's just when Molly came along things changed. I know it's probably the same for most couples."

Tom wanted to say that yes, it changed most couples – but mostly for the better. To say that Valerie didn't take to motherhood would be to grossly understate the situation. She almost had a breakdown when milk began to leak from her breasts and insisted Molly be bottle-fed. Tom didn't worry about this. He knew breastfeeding had health benefits but, after all, Molly got the nutrients she needed from formula as so many other babies did. Besides, he was able to sit in the rocking chair in the nursery and stare at his beautiful daughter while feeding her.

Valerie bemoaned the fact that her stomach would never be as flat as it had been before she got pregnant and spent every spare minute she had at the gym, hiring a nanny to look after Molly while she worked out in an attempt to erase every trace of the pregnancy. To reverse the damage, as she put it.

"Look, Val. Nothing's changed. My feelings haven't. And I don't believe for one minute that yours have either. It's just some weird reaction that you're having to my grief. You'll still be mad that I'm working every hour and not spending time with you and Molly."

"Things will be different with the money from Danny. You can cut back your hours. Maybe even take a step back altogether ..."

*"What? What did you say? What money from Danny?"* He thought he was hearing things.

"The land he left you. He told me once that he had willed the farm to you. I got onto the County Cork website and found the portfolio. You can sell it. I spoke to a few auctioneers in Cork. You can sell it. Maybe keep a small bit, say a few acres, for yourself if you want. I had a valuation done and it's worth a lot of money."

*"That – is – not – your – money.* My father left that land to me. And not even to me. He wants me to use the money for the benefit of Inchahown. Anyway, Val, our settlement is done and dusted. I bought you out of the company and I pay the mortgage on this house. Bloody hell, you're like a vulture. All of this is making sense now. The sex. The supportive wife. It was all an act! And do you know what? *I'm bloody relieved.* I thought I was losing my mind for the last few days."

# Chapter Forty-Two

"That shower in RTÉ are idiots," said Jack, walking into the bakery.

This wasn't exactly the way Kate wanted him to meet Maud, all fired up and spitting nails. She tried to cut him off at the pass.

"Honestly, they wouldn't know a good idea if it got up and bit them in the arse! How's my favourite woman in the world today?" He took Kate in his arms and planted a big kiss on her mouth.

"Jack, this is Maud. Maud, this loudmouth is Jack," said Kate.

Kate had kidnapped Maud after the funeral and brought her to Dublin. There was no way she was going to allow Maud to mope around the house feeling sorry for herself. Maud had even considered going back to Boston and Kate was afraid that if she went home to her family she might not ever see her again. Maud had been making herself useful since arriving at the shop and not for the first time, Kate wished they were still working together.

"Oh. Hello, Maud. It's nice to meet you. Sorry. I was just having a rant about our so-called national television station. I sent them a tape we made of Kate being totally delicious and they said they're not interested at the moment. Budgetary constraints or some such guff. Morons!" He shook Maud's hand.

"It's nice to meet you too," she said.

"He's not usually this manic," said Kate. "He's normally much saner than this."

"Don't apologise for him. I like a man who'll go all out for his girl. It's an admirable trait."

Kate was pleased. She wanted Maud to like Jack. She didn't have many people in her life whose opinion she valued. Her sisters wouldn't give a damn if she dated a serial killer and her friends were scattered to the four corners of the world. It would be next Christmas before she saw most of them again. She knew that her and Jack's relationship was going places and it was nice to get the nod of approval from Maud.

"That was some great work you did, Jack," said Maud. "The photoshoot, I mean. I know you had great raw material to work with but you managed to make Kate look even more gorgeous. And the cakes, oh my God! It's no wonder Kate can't keep up with the orders."

Maud thought that Kate would be fabulous on television. She had the gorgeous auburn hair, the curvaceous figure, plump lips and green eyes in the beautiful face. If RTÉ didn't want her, then Maud knew that the American or British audiences would love her. They would eat her up. She was like an Irish equivalent of Nigella Lawson. A younger, sexier version.

"Have you sent the tape to the US and UK TV food networks? I think they'd love Kate. What's not to love, right?"

"No, I haven't. Do you think it's worth a try?" asked Jack.

"Hell, yes. She could be a big star. She has it all."

꘎꘎꘎ ꘎꘎꘎

A few days later, Jack arrived into OTT Cakes. He made his way to the back of the shop where he knew Kate would be.

"Kate, Food Network UK want to meet us. Well, they want to meet you!" He was beside himself with excitement. He was jumping up and down and acting like a total eejit.

"Who? And for what?" Kate had a pain in her arm from holding the heavy piping bag at just the right angle.

"Food Network UK. They loved the demo. Their exact words were '*We think she could be the next big thing*'. There's no way they say that about every demo that crosses their desks. That's you they're talking about. Holy shit, Kate, this could be your big break."

"Not before I get this decoration finished, it won't! Jack, move it! I mean it. If this goes wrong and I have to start again, I might very well murder you."

"Well, there's gratitude for you. I work my backside off trying to get you an audition and that's the thanks I get," he said with mock hurt.

"Jack, we'll talk about it when I'm done. Now go grab a coffee or something, but let me finish. *Please.*"

The cake she was working on was taking forever. When she took the order, she hadn't anticipated just how intricate the detail was. She was so deep in concentration that she had no time to think about what Jack had just told her.

Eventually Jack got fed up waiting for her and left. He said he'd call to her flat later that night and she could thank him properly then. *Ha!* If she ever got out of the bakery, that was.

Maud had offered to stay around for a couple of days and help with the huge amount of cake orders that had built up.

"Was that Jack?" she asked as she came back to the section of the kitchen where the cakes were iced and decorated.

"Yeah. He was putting me off so I told him to go. He kept going on about the Food Network and what I should wear when we go to meet them. For fuck's sake, I couldn't even concentrate! This cake is really important."

"Hold on. Stop what you're doing for a second," said Maud.

Kate stopped mid-pipe, holding the heavy bag up with her two hands. "What?"

"The Food Network want to meet you? Is that what you're telling me?"

"Yeah. I think so. I'm not sure exactly what he said. I was too busy trying not to fuck up the icing on Bono's daugher's birthday cake."

"Do you hear yourself, Kate?"

"Yes, I do. Bono's wife ordered a cake for their daughter's birthday and they're picking it up in the morning. I have to have it finished tonight to make sure everything sets."

"Forget the cake. *The freakin' Food Network.* They want to meet you, Kate. This could be the start of an incredible career. I have a good feeling about this. You need to go for it. And give me that!" Maud took

233

the piping bag out of her hands. "Now get out of here. Find Jack and start preparing for your meteoric rise to stardom."

Kate laughed but Maud pushed her out of the prep area and ordered her again to go home.

Kate didn't have the strength to argue. She surrendered the icing into Maud's capable hands. "Thanks for being here. I don't know what I'd do without you."

⟫⟫ ⟪⟪

Jack was already at her flat. He had come down from his high and was sitting calmly on the sofa watching TV.

"I thought you were going to be there all night with that cake?" he said.

"Maud rescued me. She said she'd finish it off," she replied, kicking off her shoes.

"Come here and I'll rub your tired feet,"

Kate sat on one end of the couch and put her feet in Jack's lap. She groaned as he massaged the balls of her feet with his thumbs.

"Sorry about earlier. What were you saying about the Food Network?"

"Oh, you know. Just that they loved the demo and that they're interested in having a meeting with you."

"Oh."

"Ah, here! Is that all you can say?" Jack said, dropping her foot and sitting up straight. "This is huge. They are the biggest dedicated food channel in Europe. They have millions of viewers. You could sound a bit more excited."

"I am excited, Jack. It's just that I'm really feckin' tired. I need to go to sleep but I promise that when I wake up I'll give you and the Food Network my full attention."

# Chapter Forty-Three

The next morning Tom got a phone call from Doug.

"OK. This is a good start," said Doug, more upbeat than Tom had heard him before. "If I could've had my pick of judges, Judge Janice Armstrong would have been my first choice. She's a notorious champion of the underdog. You never know, Tom, our luck could be changing."

"I hope so. I could do with some luck right now."

He was glad that he had chosen Doug as his brief. Doug was born in the East End of London into a long line of market traders. Doug's father had different ideas for his children and was adamant that they wouldn't stand behind market stalls for their whole lives. There were similarities to Tom and his own father and Doug and Tom hit it off from their first meeting years ago.

"I know you're having a rough time right now but I need to you to stay focused. And positive," Doug said.

Tom wondered how he could be positive while facing such a formidable opponent as Gilbrade.

"I'll certainly try," he said.

"Excellent. Kick-off is a ten o'clock tomorrow morning. See you in court."

Tom thought Doug made it sound like they were off to a football game. He himself felt like he was off to the guilloutine.

⟫⟫ ⟪⟪

Tom spent the night tossing and turning. He felt like there were a million things running through his mind at the same time. He thought about Danny until the grief and the weight of how he was gambling on his inheritance almost drove him crazy. What if they lost? And there was a strong possibility that would be the case. Gilbrade could afford the best legal representation and no matter how good Doug and his team were, would they be any match for the giant pharmaceutical outfit?

And Valerie. The image of what took place in Danny's house in Inchahowen played on a loop in his head for quite a chunk of time as well. He knew that regrets were useless, that the past could not be changed, but he still couldn't help but wish it never happened.

Then there was Maud. He again saw her face in the pub after the funeral. She felt betrayed. And she was right to feel that way. He had betrayed her. The person who he saw his future with. The woman who made him believe in love again. He had messed everything up for them. She wasn't picking up his calls or answering his texts. But he knew one thing for certain, he would never give up on her.

He eventually gave up on trying to get to sleep and got out of bed at five o'clock. He made tea and sat on the sofa. He flicked the TV on and landed on a news programme about climate change. He was glad to engross himself in the plight of the polar icecaps and generally get enraged about the state of the planet. It took his mind off what was about to happen in court in a few short hours.

When the programme was over, he checked his emails and caught up on correspondence for work.

At eight he showered and got ready for court. He checked himself in the mirror before he left the flat. He was wearing his dark navy suit, white shirt and light-blue tie. He got a taxi and met Doug outside the court. There were lots of media there and Tom imagined there must be some big case going on that they were covering.

"What's with all the press? Is there a celebrity trial on?" he asked Doug.

"No. Just you. David vs. Goliath. This will have Gilbrade rattled, I can tell you. I imagine they thought they'd be in and out without being noticed. You can thank your friend Simon for this. His little article has made a big impression."

Simon York had run a piece on Gilbrade in the *Business Weekly*. It outlined Gilbrade's expansion into the Far East, to countries where labour was cheaper and environmental laws were weaker. He had included a few testimonials from workers with big mortgages who were about to lose their jobs. It wasn't exactly a love letter to the pharmaceutical company.

Inside the court, Tom and Doug saw the Gilbrade lawyers frantically on their phones when they entered the lobby. They were on to their public relations office no doubt wondering how they would spin this one.

After a couple of minutes standing around, they were informed by a court clerk that there was a delay. Tom felt him stomach lurch when Doug told him. He wanted this to be over.

"A delay? How long?"

"It's hard to know. How about we go for breakfast? There's a greasy spoon around the corner that does a wonderful Full English. I'll let the clerk know and give him my number. He can call me if we're needed."

"I don't know if I can stomach anything now, Doug," Tom said.

"Of course you can. A fried breakfast is just what the doctor ordered."

Doug and Tom walked the few hundred yards to the café. On the way, Doug declared that he had a really good feeling about how the case would go. As Tom walked along beside him, he couldn't help but be buoyed up by his counsel's sudden optimism.

They stood in line to order their food. The smell of grease was somehow comforting. It suddenly reminded Tom of Danny's fry-ups that he would make on the weekends. Father and son would sit in contented silence, after the milking the cows on a Saturday morning. Only there was no contented silence in the café.

They placed their orders and were told to take a seat and the food would be be brought to them. As soon as the plates arrived, Doug tucked in like he hadn't eaten in a week. Tom moved the bacon and sausages around his plate, barely eating a morsel.

"They're rattled by the media presence," Doug said. "They'll surely have to make some kind of statement that will protect their shareholders. Thank God for publicly traded companies!"

"I wished I could share your optimism," said Tom.

"This is way too personal for you. You've got too much at stake. Leave it to me. We'll come out of this triumphant. Now, eat up and let's go and face the music."

⤜⤜ ⤛⤛

The flashbulbs were going off in Tom's eyes as he and Doug made their way through the High Courts of Justice. He looked straight ahead, looking more focused and calm than he actually felt. He wanted everyone to see that he had done nothing wrong, that in fact a great wrong had been done to him.

Doug took him by the arm and they went in through the doors to face the judge. As they walked down the corridor, one of Gilbrade's legal team called Doug aside. Doug told Tom to wait where he was and he walked over to the window to talk to Gilbrade's lawyer. Tom could see the animated conversation but he couldn't make out what the woman was saying to Doug. They spoke for about two minutes then Doug turned and walked towards Tom.

"They'll settle," Doug said, relief emanating from his every pore.

Tom was stunned. "*What?* What does that mean exactly? I thought the reason we were here is because they didn't want to settle? Does this mean no hearing?" The words tumbled out of his mouth at full speed.

"They want you to drop the case. They're in talks with their insurance company to see what kind of settlement they can make. But you can bet your bottom dollar that it'll be big. It will be enough to cover all your costs. And extra to compensate you for their cancellation of the project. This is good news, Tom!"

Tom's facial expression was still one of consternation and disbelief. "You mean it's over?"

"It is. You just have to sit back and wait for the money to roll in."

⤜⤛ ⤚⤛

Tom sat in his flat that evening and poured himself a large whiskey. Earlier in the day he had gathered all the staff together. They were mightily relieved that their jobs were safe. It was a great feeling to see the joy the news brought to all of his colleagues. But there was something niggling at him. The Gilbrade debacle was a watershed moment in his life. He was sure that there were lessons to be learned. There was the obvious lesson of doing better due diligence when taking on a project, but it wasn't just that. He felt like there was a life lesson in there somewhere too. What was he doing? Did he want to do what he was doing for the rest of his life? Was he meant for something more? Something completely different?

# Chapter Forty-Four

Maud read through the orders that Kate had for the following week. Kate was busy decorating a wedding cake for a society wedding – a market that she wanted to dominate.

"That's a lot of orders," Maud said, putting down the sheet of paper.

"I know! It's crazy. I don't know how I'll get it all done."

"You'll have to start saying no," said Maud.

"Ha-ha. From the woman who never said 'no' to a cake order in her life. How the tables have turned!" Kate joked, fully aware that the level of work she was required to do was anything but funny.

"Kate, I need to talk to you," Maud said.

"Sounds serious."

"Well, it is. It's the offer to meet the Food Network people."

"Look, Maud. You might as well stop right there. I'm up to my eyeballs as it is. I can't take on another project at this point. Have you and Jack been talking behind my back?"

"Yes, in fact we have. Don't get mad with Jack. He hasn't told me anything I don't already know."

"So? What do you both think is best for me? Because obviously I can't trust my own judgement."

"I think you should do it. If the meeting doesn't go well or you don't like what they're offering, then fine. But if they do want to make a show with you, it could be life-changing. I mean it, Kate. I have a feeling about this. I think you're going to be the face of baking in Ireland. And the UK. The world even."

"Go away out of that! Anyway, I can't walk out on OTT. The lease has another six months to run and I still owe you the money you loaned me to start up. No. It's not the time."

"Don't let any of that stop you. I have plenty of contacts from my time at Le Cordon Bleu. I imagine there will be plenty of people who would be interested in taking over while you're gone. If not, you can find somebody else here in Dublin. Or else, you can pay the penalty to break the lease. If the Food Network deal works out, you'll be in a position to repay all your debts in no time."

"But ..."

"No buts, Kate. Just go meet them. See what they're offering. See what you think of the whole set-up. Go find out what you're actually going to be turning down."

⟫⟫ ⟪⟪

Kate and Jack walked out onto Trafalgar Square, straight from their meeting with the Food Network executives. They looked at each other and looked away again. They were unable to speak. They went into a small coffee shop and sat opposite each other, looking at the menu.

When the waitress asked them what they wanted to order, they apologised to her, put the menus down and walked out into the spring sunshine. Jack started to walk back towards the hotel and Kate followed him. The noises of London were happening outside their heads. They were in a bubble where no outside influences could reach them. Kate walked directly to the elevator while Jack stopped at the reception desk.

Kate took off her coat and shoes as she walked through the suite. She went into the bathroom and turned on the spotlight over the "His and Hers" sinks. The harsh light highlighted every bit of her face but she didn't recognise herself. She took off her clothes and donned the fluffy robe the hotel provided for its guests. She heard Jack come back into the room, using his key card.

When she walked out of the bathroom he was sitting on the edge of his side of the bed. Kate walked over to her side and sat down too. Jack started to laugh. Kate turned her head to look at him and started to laugh too. They laughed so hard she thought she might never stop. The laughing only abated when there was a rap at the door.

Jack answered. The waiter entered their room, carrying a tray with a bottle of Moet et Chandon and two glasses.

"Sir, madam, will that be all?" asked the waiter.

"Yes, thank you," said Jack, giving the waiter a fifty. A bloody fifty.

"Thank you, sir. Very kind," the waiter said, reversing himself out of the suite.

Jack popped the cork and poured two glasses. He held out one to Kate. She took a sip and started to giggle again. Jack started too. They both fell into fits of laughter, the champagne sloshing in their glasses.

"What the hell just happened?" asked Kate.

"You just got your own show on the Food Network, that's what just happened. And not only did you get your own show, they've optioned a second series before the first one has even been filmed. Hold on. Actually, you better pinch me. I'm not sure that did really happen. I'm not just dreaming this, am I?"

"No, I'm pretty sure I heard that too. *Kate Bakes*, Food Network's hottest new show," Kate said in her best British accent. "*Kate Bakes*, Bringing Sexy Back to Baking. Was sexy ever gone? Was it even there in the first place?"

"It doesn't matter where it was. It's coming back and you're bringing it. I told you, didn't I? I said you'd be a star. I knew it when I saw you through the lens the first time. They knew it when they saw the demo too. They wouldn't have put us up in this hotel, this suite, if they weren't serious about signing you. This bed is almost the size of my entire flat."

"Do you know what we should do? We should go into RTÉ with loads of Food Network bags and say 'Big Mistake'. You know, like Julia Roberts did in *Pretty Woman*," and they both laughed all over again at the thought of it.

"Some poor producer will probably get his P45 because of this. Serves him bloody right!"

"How is all of this possible? Things like this don't happen to people like me," Kate said, taking another gulp of her champagne.

"If by people like you, you mean beautiful, voluptuous goddesses? I think you'll find they do."

"Go way out of that! Voluptuous goddess, my arse! Jesus, I'll be getting a swelled head if you keep that up."

"You are. To me, you're the most beautiful creature in the world. Every time I see you all I think about is ripping your clothes off."

"So what's stopping you now?" she said, dropping her empty glass on the carpet and pulling him down on the huge bed.

# Chapter Forty-Five

In the months that followed, Kate was everywhere. She was in demand from radio stations, newspapers and TV. Word had spread about the auburn-haired beauty who had landed her own TV show on the Food Network and everybody wanted a piece of her.

Maud was still looking after things at the Bakery but she was getting restless. She wanted to be back looking out at the sea. She reasoned with herself that she was ready to go home. She had organised a local woman to go in and clean her house from top to bottom. She had organised for new bed linen to be delivered and the old ones thrown out. She didn't want any trace of Tom left behind. She didn't want to wake up smelling him off a pillow in case it send her spiralling back into a pit of misery. She wanted to be sure her future was a Tom Kennedy-free zone.

"Just a few more days. Please, Maud. I have to advertise for someone and I want you to help me interview," Kate pleaded with her friend. "I know you've done so much for me already and I wouldn't ask, but I really need you."

"OK. Just two more weeks. Then I'm outta here. Not that I didn't enjoy it but I have this hankering to go home."

"And Inchahowen is definitely home then?" asked Kate.

"Yes. No doubt in my mind at all." Maud's heart was in the tiny seaside village. Her soul was connected to the sea and the landscape. She had done all her empire-building already. She was done with big cities for now.

"You're really going to be happy with the coffee shop? That's going to be enough for you? I mean, I know there's nothing wrong with just wanting a coffee shop but it's just, you know, you had it before on a much grander scale. I don't get it."

"God, Kate. You sound like my mom. Why does everyone worry about me living in Inchahowen? It's perfect for me. I'm thinking about opening a cookery school actually. I've been giving it quite a bit of thought lately."

"I knew it! I *knew* you couldn't go back to making birthday cakes for three-year-olds. You're too talented for that. Is it going to be like Ballymaloe Cookery School? They have people coming from all over the world."

"It's going to be better than Ballymaloe. It's going to be Ireland's equivalent of Le Cordon Bleu."

"You're setting the bar pretty high for yourself, so. Nothing new there, I suppose. I know it'll be a huge success. Only for you, I wouldn't be where I am now. I'd probably still be sitting in an office somewhere wondering why I was miserable. If you can teach others what you taught me, you'll be onto a winner straight away."

"*Aw shucks*, Kate, you're making me blush," she laughed. "Don't underestimate your own talent. Even without me, I'm pretty sure you'd have discovered your passion." After all, Kate had made it, despite all of the obstacles which were put in her path.

"What about, well, you know?" asked Kate.

"What?"

"Sex. Love. I've got bad news for you – I don't think you're going to meet the love of your life in Inchahowen, cookery school or not."

"So you're saying if I move back to Inchahowen, I might never have sex again," said Maud, laughing.

"Yes, I'm afraid there is a distinct possibility that will be the case," said Kate with mock seriousness.

"Well, that's fine with me. Maybe I don't want to have sex ever again. I'm over men. I'm going to concentrate on building my business not on falling in love, so you don't have to worry about me."

"But you can't just give up on love. That bloody cousin of mine, twice removed, needs his head examined. I don't know how he could choose her over you. I really don't. I apologise on behalf of my whole family," said Kate, still flabbergasted at Tom's behaviour.

"Don't. It's better for their little girl. She deserves to have her mom and dad. It's the only thing that makes sense about all of this. Anyway it's not exactly a hardship for Tom to be married to Valerie. She's beautiful." Maud remembered seeing her the day of the funeral and the way she put her hand on Tom's shoulder possessively. She had to let it go. Like she had to let Tom go.

# Chapter Forty-Six

Tom packed the photographs of Molly into a cardboard box. There were other bits and pieces that he would take with him. The decision to leave London had been an easy one in the end. Once he had started questioning his mission in life, all roads pointed to Inchahowen. Gilbrade had taught him a hard lesson. One that he had learned from and hopefully moved on from too.

The partners in the firm were understanding of his decision though they didn't want him to go. Tom was the face of Kennedy Architects as well as being the name over the door. But Tom had faith in the other directors and the partners and knew that the company was in good hands. He would stay on as a director but work on a consultancy basis only.

~≫⫸ ⫷≪~

Tom had called to see Valerie to inform her of his decision to move back to Ireland. He needed to revisit the issue of access. He hoped that Valerie would agree to him having Molly for school holidays at the very least. He also hoped to travel to London every two weeks to spend time with his precious daughter.

"You want to take my daughter away from me?" she asked.

"What? No. I want to see her because she's my daughter and I love her."

Valerie looked at him and Tom could feel her stare burning into his core.

"I only had her because you wanted a child, you know," she said.

"Why are you saying this, Val? I know you love Moll."

"I do love her. But I know that given the choice again, I'd chose never to have a child."

Tom couldn't believe his ears. "Why are you telling me this? I can't leave Molly with you, knowing that you'd prefer that she wasn't even born."

"I've been offered a job in Hong Kong."

"A job? Doing what?"

Valerie hadn't worked since Tom met her. She had worked as a design consultant for Harvey Nicholls once but that was only for a short stint and when she was in her early twenties. She spent most of her time on committees raising funds for charities and quaffing champagne at fundraising dinners.

"Running an art gallery. Someone I met at the party on Boxing Day. Hugo Bennett. He's an art dealer. He owns galleries all over the world." She said his name as if Tom should know who she was talking about.

He was probably famous in Valerie's circle but Tom didn't have a clue who this Hugo guy was.

"And what about Molly? There is no way you're taking her to Hong Kong. Over my dead body!"

"That's the thing, Tom. I don't want to take her. I want her to live with you."

Tom noticed that she had the good grace to look ashamed by her admission.

"Of course she must live with me! Especially when you've said all those vile things about not wanting her."

Valerie wrung her hands. "I don't blame you for hating me."

Tom looked at his ex-wife. She was a child. A baby herself. She had never taken the time to grow up and become an adult with all the associated shit that goes with it.

"I don't hate you, Val. I do feel sorry for you though. Molly is an amazing girl. If you're not careful, you'll wake up one day and you'll have missed out on so much joy."

"Don't turn her against me," she said, her voice cracking.

"I love Molly way too much to do that to her," Tom said. "I want her to grow up believing that she is truly loved by her daddy and her mummy. And that's what I'll tell her."

⋙ ⋘

There were some final loose ends that need to be tied up before Tom could fly back to Ireland. He had tried to reach Maud but she continued to ignore his calls and texts. He had even tried the coffee shop but whoever was running the shop for her was not giving her whereabouts away to anybody. On one occasion he had pretended to be a sales rep from one of the catering companies but the guy had just politely asked for his number and said he would get Maud to call him back. She didn't.

⇶ ⇇

"Are we going to Grandpa Danny's house?" Molly asked as she packed her little bits and pieces into a pink rucksack that Tom told her she could bring on the aeroplane. He had packed a suitcase with all of her clothes and some of the bigger toys that wouldn't be considered hand luggage. Molly was busy tying the zip on her little pink bag and Tom could see her tongue sticking out while she concentrated with all her might on closing the zip on the overstuffed bag.

He felt a pang of something. He wasn't quite sure. Then he remembered his mother. Rose. The way her tongue stuck out while she concentrated on some task or other. Peeling potatoes. Darning socks. Setting the fire. Molly looked like her, he realised. Why had he never seen it before? Why had he not seen a lot of things before? Because he had been locked in battle with Valerie for years, that's why. Because when he was finished fighting Valerie, he'd had to fight Gilbrade. He was fighting grief. He was fighting love. He was tired of fighting. He wanted to take his little girl home.

# Chapter Forty-Seven

Maud was glad to be home. The contract cleaners she had hired had meticulously scrubbed the cottage from top to bottom. Not a trace of Tom was left behind. She imagined that now Danny was gone that Tom would have no reason to come back to Inchahowen. She could get on with her life, safe in the knowledge that she would never see him again.

However, a constant reminder of Danny, and therefore Tom, was the presence of Ned who had made up his mind to move in with her – but she appreciated the company, even if it was the four-legged variety.

She was glad of the distraction of starting the cookery school and had started to put a few ideas down on paper. A trip to the local planning office was necessary if she was to get the project off the ground. There were marvellous cookery schools dotted all around Ireland but Maud wanted hers to be the best. Plain and simple. She took her rough drawings and drove to the planning office for her appointment with the head planner.

"Have you studied the plan for the general area?" asked the planner who looked like she should still be in high school.

"Actually, no, I haven't. I wasn't aware there was a general plan. May I see it?" asked Maud. As far as Maud could remember, nobody had applied to build anything other than the odd house in Inchahowen for years. The planning in the area was haphazard to say the least and she wondered if any of the houses in the area had actually had planning permission at all.

"You certainly can. Come with me."

Maud followed the planner to the public area where she showed Maud an application and plans for a golf resort and hotel. Maud was amazed. Who the hell was thinking about putting a hotel in Inchahowen? It was barely on the map and could hardly be considered a destination. It was a place of extreme beauty but being so remote and uninhabited made it more so. Maud almost laughed at how ridiculous it was. Surely there wasn't a snowball's chance in hell this planning monstrosity would get the green light.

"Oh my God! What kind of person thinks this is a good idea?" Maud asked the teen planner.

"The council does for a start," the planner said indignantly. "We've given the go-ahead for the development already. It's in keeping with the county plan and it will have huge benefits for the local community."

Maud couldn't believe it. And then she realised. The land for the proposed site was Danny's land. What was going on?

"May I ask who put in the application?" said Maud. Maybe it wasn't too late to launch some kind of objection. Surely there would still be time for that?

"It's there on the plans," said the child planner, pointing to the drawings. *"Tom Kennedy of Kennedy Architects."*

Tom? *Christ.* More evidence if she needed it, that she didn't know him at all. She cursed herself for being a stupid fool.

The planner excused herself and drifted off in another direction, leaving Maud to try to digest the news that Inchahowen was to be transformed into some kind of Disneyland for golfers. And Tom Kennedy was the one who was going to make it happen.

*✸✸✸ ❧❧❧*

"It's there on the plans," said the child planner, pointing to the drawings. *"Daniel John Kennedy and Tom Kennedy. It's a joint application."*

Danny? Surely not. This had to be all down to Tom. More evidence if she needed it, that she didn't know him at all. She cursed herself for being a stupid fool. The planner excused herself and drifted off in another direction, leaving Maud to try to digest the news that Inchahowen was to be transformed into some kind of Disneyland for golfers.

*✸✸✸ ❧❧❧*

Later that day in the coffee shope, Eileen Gaffney was in having a skinny latte with her friend Eithne Kelly. As Maud dropped off their coffees, she heard them discuss the proposed plans for the hotel and golf course.

"There'll be somewhere else to have your coffee soon. The new hotel," said Maud.

"I know. Isn't it wonderful?" Eileen said excitedly. "But, oh no, we'll still come here for the coffee, don't worry. But it will be a great addition to the village. Imagine, our very own hotel!"

"I can't wait," chimed in Eithne.

What the hell? Maud imagined the town would be up in arms at such a development. She must be missing something. She tried another angle.

"It will completely change the look and feel of the village. It's so perfect the way it is," she said wistfully.

"Perfect, my eye!" said Eileen. "The place is dying on its feet. Mark my words, it'll be the makin' of the area. We won't know ourselves. It won't be one of those awful glass-and- concrete monstrosities like they have some places either. It'll a lovely design, I'm sure. If Tom's half as good an architect as Danny said he was."

Tom was to be the architect! Maud winced like she'd been hit by some physical pain How would she cope knowing he was in close proximity but not able to be with him? She reminded herself that she had coped with worse things in her life.

"And the jobs," continued Eithne. "Sure there's no young people left at all hardly. At least they'll be able to stay now if they want to. There's going to be a hundred jobs, so I hear. Ah, fair play to Tom. And to Danny! He's left a hell of a legacy behind, that's for sure."

Maud had to admit defeat. Eileen and Eithne were the best judges of what the community was thinking. They were in the thick of everything. Well, everything there was to be in the thick of in Inchahowen. They were in the Women's Club, the Rotary Club and were the also well in with Father O'Brien. Maud wondered if Tom had somehow put a spell on the whole community. How else could this wave of goodwill towards his development have been possible?

# Chapter Forty-Eight

Maud was so used to seeing Kate's beautiful face online and on the front pages of magazines that she barely took any notice any more. When she saw Kate's picture online, she imagined she would be reading more about Kate's meteoric rise and her celebrity status. It took her a few seconds to process the headline:

**Kate Bakes – Kate's Abusive Alco Father Horror**

*Sisters break their silence*

*Abusive alco father horror?* Maud scrolled until she found the article. Or the promise of an article. It said that Kate's sisters were going to reveal a life of childhood hell. Holy shit! Kate was in the UK doing promotional work for her show. She was going down a storm if the Food Network's social media was anything to go by. She also regularly appeared on TV promoting *Kate Bakes*.

Maud needed to talk to her. She called her mobile and wondered what the hell she was going to say. The phone rang out so Maud tried Jack's number.

"Maud. Hi. Is everything OK?" Jack said in a sleepy voice.

"No, not exactly. Is Kate with you?"

"No, she's gone to the gym. I'm just catching a few extra zeds."

"Look, Jack, I don't what is going on or where they got this, but there's a headline in *Today Magazine Online*. It says that they're going to feature a story about Kate's dad being an abusive alcoholic. Do you have any idea what that could be about?"

"*Abusive alcoholic?* No. Kate doesn't say much about him. She did say he was a big drinker alright. Does it mention what kind of abuse?" Jack was fully awake now.

"No, it just mentions her sisters," said Maud.

"What does it say about them?"

"It says that the story is coming from them. In their own words kind of thing."

"*Fuck,*" Jack said.

"If the media in the UK get onto this, some journalist could ambush Kate and ask her something during an interview or even doorstep her at the gym. Depending on how she answers, she could be kissing her new career goodbye. I think she needs to get in touch with her sisters and find out exactly what they've told that goddamn magazine."

After the call, Maud sat there wondering. She knew that Kate had a hard upbringing. She had told Maud about her father's chronic drinking and how her mother had died when they were so young. Maud had nothing but huge admiration for Kate for making something of herself despite the upbringing the girls got. This revelation, whatever it was, could wreck everything she had worked for.

Maud hoped it wasn't true. Maybe Emer and Grace made up the story for the money. Maud knew that they were victims too. They just didn't have the desire to succeed that Kate had. It was very possible that they were jealous of Kate's success and wanted somehow to cash in on it. Maud had made up her mind that there was no abuse, that her sisters had just wanted to make a quick buck at their famous sister's expense.

# Chapter Forty-Nine

Kate walked up the path to Emer's front door. The garden was handkerchief-sized but neat as a new pin. She banged so hard on the glass that she almost put her fist through it.

"What the fuck is all this about?" fumed Kate, waving a screenshot on her phone at her sister when she opened the door.

"Well, hello to you too," said Emer, standing back and letting her sister into the house.

Maud had been right. The salacious headline had been picked up by all the daily newspapers and it had even been referred to in one of the national news bulletins. Kate and Jack were contacted immediately by the Food Network's PR people to see what could be done to limit the damage done. They advised Kate to go back to Ireland and sort it out. Nobody wanted *Kate Bakes* to be tainted with anything as undesirable as abuse. Of any sort.

Kate had done her best to convince the network executives that there was absolutely no truth in it, only vicious rumour. She didn't say that it was most likely her gold-digger sisters trying to make a few quid for themselves which she was convinced was the case.

She had flown back to Ireland straight away to confront Emer and Grace head on.

"I think we can dispense with niceties, don't you? We're way beyond that. What exactly were you thinking? What's it all about? If you need money you could have asked me straight out."

"*Ha*," said Emer.

"*Ha?* Is that it? You're ruining my career and that's all you can fucking-well say for yourself? Jesus Christ, I could fucking *kill* you!"

"I don't want your money. Grace doesn't want it either. For all we care you can shove your money and your career up your hole."

"Charming, thanks. Well, if it's not about money what is it about? I'm sorry, I'm at a complete loss here. What kind of abuse hell did we live in? Am I missing something? Yes, our father was a chronic alcoholic and an absolute fucking bastard to boot. We were poor, we weren't loved like we should have been. *Boo-hoo!* But abuse? That's low. Did you actually tell a reporter that we were abused? Did you actually say those words? Please tell me that your words were twisted and taken out of context just so the magazine could get a good story."

"I want Grace to be here," said Emer, dialling her sister's number.

Grace lived nearby and Emer offered Kate a cup of tea while they were waiting for her to arrive.

"No, thank you." Kate looked around her sister's kitchen. It was clean and tidy. She hadn't given much thought to her sisters' lives but she had imagined they would be living in much the same conditions that they had lived in when they were young.

She was glad for Kylie, Emer's daughter. There were toys around the place too. Lovely toys, all neatly stacked in coloured plastic boxes at one end of the room.

Grace arrived within minutes. She let herself into the house. The two sisters were always close. Kate was always the one set apart. She was four years younger than Grace and five younger than Emer. Kate wished she had sisters who she could have a fun relationship with. Go away for weekends to Paris with. Sisters who could share in her successes. But they had chosen to go down a different road and made it clear that they didn't want anything to do with her.

"Kate's wondering why we just didn't ask her for money instead of selling our story to that magazine," said Emer to Grace.

"*Ha!*" said Grace.

Jesus, had these women no vocabulary, thought Kate. "Ah, seriously! It would be nice if you said more than just '*ha!*'. I have a show that's due to air in a few weeks and this is a major pain in my ass. So if you wouldn't mind contacting the reporter and saying that it was a misunderstanding – that there was no abuse. Yes, he was a terrible alco, but he never abused us. Then we can all get on with our lives."

"You're such a spoiled little bitch," said Emer. "You always were. Everything was always about you. You think you're better than us. Always looking down your nose at us for staying in Inchahowen. Thinking you're better with your big job and your fancy shop. But who did you call when you got yourself into trouble?"

"Yeah, you came running to us to send Doc and Haystack to sort you out. Why didn't you ask your fancy friends? I suppose they wouldn't get their hands dirty," said Grace.

"I don't think I'm better than you," said Kate. "I don't know where you get that idea from. You chose to not to have careers. I chose to work hard in school and go to college. You could've done that too. There was nothing stopping you doing exactly what I did."

"Don't make me laugh!" said Emer. "You think we could have gone off to college and left you behind with *him*? Maybe we should've, Grace. Maybe we should've pissed off and left her. What would her life be like now if we did that, do you think?"

"But we never would've done it – never," said Grace sadly.

"Why? Why not? You girls are smart. I have to say you didn't make very smart choices, but it's not too late. You can still make something of your lives," said Kate, immediately regretting her condescending tone.

Her sisters huffed and puffed and Kate thought she might be on the receiving end of a dig from Grace like she had been many times in her childhood.

"Choices? Fucking choices? We didn't have choices. If we weren't there, he woulda done it to you," said Grace.

"Done what? What are you talking about?" said Kate, alarmed by Grace's serious tone.

"He woulda touched you, he woulda, he woulda gone into your room. Like he did with us. Why do you think I slept in the room with you? He was doing it to us. Well, mainly to Emer but to me too sometimes. We were minding you. You were only small. He was

265

a fucking pig. A monster. He did it to us until we were big enough to fight him off."

A silence fell in the kitchen. The three sisters sat around the kitchen table. They each looked at their hands folded on the table.

Kate's heart was thudding from the shock. She wanted to shout at them and call them liars but she knew deep down that they weren't lying. She remembered the miserable house they grew up in. The thickness of the air. The constant fear. The presence of the unspoken evil. She wanted to rip the skin off her arms to somehow try to shed the person who lived in that house of horrors. She remembered only angry voices from her childhood. She never brought friends home because she knew that normal people didn't live like they did.

Kate looked around again and saw toys and comfort and wondered how Emer had managed to survive the abuse and come out the other side, capable of loving her own child.

Emer was trying hard not to cry. Grace put a hand on her arm.

Kate felt like she couldn't join in. They had their own thing going on. Kate had always put it down to their age but, in fact, it was because they were keeping this huge monstrous secret. She had never felt so humbled in her life. These two women, who Kate had spent her adult life trying to get away from, were in fact her saviours. Her life could have turned out so much differently if these two brave women, who were only girls at the time, hadn't stood between her and evil.

Suddenly tears were rolling down her cheeks. "I ... I don't know what ... I'm sorry ... I'm sorry that happened to you," she sobbed.

Emer and Grace looked at her and nodded their heads.

"I don't know how to thank you for protecting me. I don't know ..." Kate couldn't continue.

Her life's beliefs were skewed. She had gone through life thinking that nobody loved her. But what else could describe what Emer and Grace had done except as an act of love? Not only had they saved her from the same fate as theirs but they had also tended to him when he was sick and dying. Kate had bullied them into visiting him every day.

"I made you go there every day. Why didn't you tell me then? I had a right to know. *For fuck's sake, I would've killed him myself!*"

"We never wanted you to know. The reporter caught us off guard. She asked us about him and we said he was had a drink problem and all that. Then she said she'd been told he had abused us. I think now that she was talking about him hittin' us but Grace, the feckin' genius, piped up and said 'Yeah, but he never touched Kate *blah blah blah!*' I nearly killed her with a look but it was too late. Yer one latched on to it and wouldn't let it go. We didn't give any details but she had enough to be off and runnin' with her story."

"I don't give a shite about the reporter!" Kate cried. "Why didn't you tell me when I was finished college at least? I nursed that bastard. I spoon-fed him like a bloody baby. I would have left him there to die if I knew what he did to you. And I definitely wouldn't have blamed you if you never went near him while he was dying!"

"Don't worry, we made him suffer," said Emer. "We used to tell him he was a pervert and all. We made sure he understood what we were saying. We never laid a hand on him physically but we told him he was going straight to hell to burn with all the other evil pricks in the world.

I'm pretty sure he didn't see any white light when he died, only a big raging furnace. Serves the fucker right!"

Kate couldn't imagine what her sisters had been through. She didn't want to imagine the horror of their father getting into their bed and taking advantage of their innocence. Emer was always such a miserable cow but it was no wonder. The same Emer who had her spick and span house and her daughter. She wondered if ...

"Is Kylie ...? Is ...?" Kate muttered.

"Kylie is Haystack's. He, our da, stopped doing 'it' by then," said Emer. If I'da got pregnant by that bastard, I'd have ripped the child from my own body." She almost retched at the thought. "The only person who kept me sane when all of that was going on was Haystack. Even me and Grace couldn't really talk about it. Haystack probably saved my life. I thought about killin' meself, but I was afraid Da would go after you two."

"Does Haystack know?" asked Kate.

"No. I told him that he was rough with us. I told him that he was a drunk and that I was scared of him. He and Doc offered to burn the house down with him in it. I almost took them up on it but I was afraid they'd get caught."

Kate now wished he had burned it down. She hated her father. She never liked him, only felt a sense of duty to him. She wished that she had let him die roaring. She wished that she hadn't fed him and cleaned him. She wished most of all that the three sisters had been lucky enough to be born to parents who actually wanted them.

"I'm sorry, Emer. If I had known I wouldn't have let ... I wouldn't have ... I don't know what I would have done. I know I couldn't have done what you did for us. I didn't deserve it, the way I treated you. I'm so sorry."

She put her face in her hands and cried like she hadn't cried since she was a child. She had thought she was immune to crying. Growing up in her house made her tough and she had never come across a circumstance that had warranted tears. Until now. She felt she might never stop. She wasn't crying about her career which was on the cusp of being ruined. She was crying for the love she never knew existed. The love her sisters had for her all along. She had gone to Dublin and never looked back. When she left, she didn't care if she never saw them again. Yet when she was in trouble, they were the only people she could call. She didn't know then that they loved her but she knew it now. Emer was standing over her now and had her arms around her. How she was capable of any kindness, Kate didn't know.

"It's over, Kate," Emer said. "He's gone. And he's gone knowing that he was an evil bastard. He's rotting in hell as we're sitting here. Doesn't that make you feel better about things?"

"I suppose," said Kate.

Emer, letting her go, put a box of tissues in front of her and sat down again. Kate took some tissues and dried her face.

"What about counselling? Did you have any?" she asked then.

"Yeah, but we didn't find it much use, to be honest," said Emer. "Your one was tellin' us that it wasn't our fault. Sure we feckin' know that. He was a bastard. We were his kids. It was awful what happened but it did happen and we can't just pretend it didn't and that everything's rosy in the garden."

Kate once again marvelled at her sisters' attitude.

"We're still going to counselling though," said Grace.

Kate was glad.

"I feel really bad about talking to the reporter," said Grace. "You see, I blurted that out cos I thought she actually knew and I was trying to protect you and say it was nothing to do with you. That was stupid – I shoulda just denied it all, of course. You know we never told anyone and didn't mean to ever let anyone know. What happened is private. We didn't want it plastered all over the papers. People pointing at us and feeling sorry for us. And Kylie. Especially Kylie. I don't want her knowin' anything."

"So what will we do?" asked Kate.

"We'll just deny everything. Just say that the reporter must have made it up. She's meant to be comin' back on Friday to record the interview. I'll tell her there's nothing to record. I'll tell her she must've been on drugs or somethin' if she thought I said anything about abuse."

"Do you think that will work?" asked Kate hopefully. She wanted to tell the world that she had the best sisters anybody could ask for but she didn't want their horror spread across newspapers for the public's delectation.

"If we all keep *shtum*, they won't have a story, will they?" said Grace.

"Thank you. Thank you both for everything," said Kate.

# Chapter Fifty

Kate rang Maud's doorbell.

"Hey, stranger!" said Maud, as Ned wagged an enthusiastic welcome. "It's odd to see you back in Inchahowen."

"Can I come in?"

"Of course," said Maud, stepping aside.

Kate flopped down on the big sofa, looking like she'd been to hell and back.

Maud was alarmed. "You OK?" she asked.

"The abuse. It happened. They weren't telling lies."

"You mean like it said in the magazine?" asked Maud, horrified. Like Kate, she assumed it was the lazy sisters' way of making a few bucks. She never in her wildest dreams thought it might be for real. "Jesus Christ, Kate. How? I mean ..."

Ned leapt up on the couch and sat staring anxiously at Kate.

"They protected me, Maud. All this time, I thought they were lazy, sitting on their fat arses, good-for-nothings. But they actually saved me. Our father . . . he abused them. They let him do it to them so that he wouldn't do it to me. Grace slept in my bed for my whole childhood just so she could protect me. When he came into our bedroom . . ."

Kate was in floods of tears by now and could barely finish her sentence, "Grace got out of bed and went with him and let him . . ."

Maud felt the horror of what happened. Poor Kate. And her sisters. They were only kids.

Poor Ned was going around in circles on the couch, trying to make Kate stop crying. He did the same thing when Maud cried at night. Maud moved Ned out of the way and sat next to Kate and held her tightly under his watchful gaze.

"I'm so sorry," said Maud, holding Kate's shaking frame. "*Shhhh ... shhhhh ...* It's going to be alright. He's gone now. He can't harm any of you anymore."

"I wish he was still alive. I want to tell him what I think of what he did. I want to scream at him and kick the shite out of him. I want to hurt him, Maud. I want to make him as fucking scared as he made my sisters."

Maud let her rant. She needed to get it all out. When eventually Kate's tears subsided, Maud made tea. She handed a mug to Kate who looked exhausted. She had flown from London and then drove straight to her sisters' house on only a couple of hours' sleep.

Maud could see that she could barely hold the mug in her shaking hand. Maud started to plump up pillows and went upstairs to get a quilt. She herself had spent many, many nights on this couch and she knew that Kate would sleep like a baby.

Kate allowed Maud to take off her shoes and lay down on the comfortable sofa. She allowed Maud to cover her in the softest down duvet which felt like millions of silky feathers enveloping her. Ned lay down on the floor against the couch, letting her know that he was minding her too.

⤛⤜

"Why did you let me sleep for so long?" asked Kate the following morning.

"You needed it. Here, I've made you a cuppa," said Maud, noting that Kate still managed to look beautiful despite no make-up and creased clothes.

Kate took the cup gratefully and blew on it before sipping the hot tea.

"I'm making pancakes. What do you want on them?"

"Maud, you're too good to me," Kate said, getting off the sofa and moving to the kitchen table where there was butter, lemons, sugar and Nutella to choose from.

Maud put a plate with two pancakes on front of Kate.

Kate went for lemon and sugar and tucked in hungrily.

Maud loved how Kate ate with gusto. She loved food and that's what made the executives love her too.

"How are you feeling now?" asked Maud.

"Like I want to pull that quilt back over my head and never come out again. And I'm the lucky one. He didn't touch me. I can't even begin to imagine how Emer and Grace cope every day. How do they get out of bed, put one foot in front of the other and keep going? I think I'd have gone insane by now."

"I never thought I'd say this, but you're a lucky girl to have two sisters like that," said Maud with a smile.

"I need to make it up to them somehow. I feel so humbled that they did that for me. All I ever did was tell them how pathetic they were for not being ambitious like me. Jesus Christ, I need to eat a lot of humble pie. Talking of humble pie, when are you going to open your cookery school?" Kate was worn out from thinking about the unspeakable things her father had done to her sisters and needed a change of subject.

"That's gone out the window, I'm afraid. I went to the planning office and there's an application for planning permission to build a golf resort, hotel and spa. An overcrowded tourist spot isn't exactly the location I had in mind for the school."

"Oh yeah, I heard that. Emer and Grace told me Danny left the land to be used for the benefit of the village. And that Tom is going to come up with some amazing plans for the area."

"I know, right. It's terrible."

"What? No. It's great. Genius, in fact. It's exactly what Inchahowen is crying out for."

Maud stared at her. "I can't believe it! I seem to be the only person who's against this monstrosity being built in such a beautiful place!"

"Ah, Maud! You've got to admit that this place is fucked. There are no jobs and no prospects for anybody who wants to stay around here. This way there'll be jobs. Career opportunities even. I'm sorry you're so upset by it, but I think it's wonderful."

"But do you think it's really what Danny would have wanted Tom to do?" argued Maud, unable to let it go. "Would he have wanted to turn Inchahowen into the Jersey Shore?"

"Yes, I think he would've, in fact. He hated that Tom had to go away to work and he left all that land to Tom in the hope that he'd do something with it. I think Danny would be pleased. Oh, by the way, Jack asked me to marry him."

"What? Oh my God, Kate! That's the best news!" said Maud, getting up and giving her a hug.

"But I doubt he'll still want to marry me when I tell him about my background."

"Jack isn't like that, Kate. You know it. And he loves you so much that I imagine if you told him you murdered somebody, he'd think you were completely justified."

# Chapter Fifty-One

Kate couldn't take her eyes off the Atlantic Ocean. She wondered how Maud ever managed to leave the house. The ocean changed every moment, showing her some other wonderful trick. Waves crashed and lapped, the sea turned from grey to blue to aquamarine right before her eyes.

It was only when Jack's jeep pulled up the driveway that she dragged her gaze away. Kate wished she could put this off. She wished she could send Jack away and never tell him what had happened in her home when she was a child. But things weren't that easy now. Jack had declared his love for her and proposed marriage. And she had accepted. She loved him and she owed it to him to give him an "out".

"What is it?" Jack said as soon as she opened the door.

"Come in and sit down. I need to talk to you."

"Sounds serious," he said, taking a seat on the big couch, hardly noticing Ned in his distress.

"The abuse. Emer and Grace. It happened. My father abused sexually them for years. It ..."

Kate was in tears again. She thought she had cried her all her tears the day before but there seemed to be no sign of being at the end of the well.

Jack sat rigid on the couch. Kate could see his knuckles were white with rage. She was sure that he wanted to kill her father too. He'd have to go to the end of a pretty long line.

"What about you?" he said.

"No. They protected me. They let him abuse them so that he wouldn't do it to me."

"That's pretty amazing."

"It is," agreed Kate.

"They must love you a lot."

This set Kate off again. Jack moved over and took her in his arms. He hated that anybody had caused his Kate pain. He had never seen her upset before and he didn't like it. He wanted to take all of her pain away but he knew that he wasn't that powerful.

When Maud had called him about the headline, he had a niggling feeling that he couldn't let go. In his experience, there was rarely smoke without there being a fire somewhere close by. Kate had told him about her alcoholic father and he hated that she hadn't been cherished as a young child like she should have been. It was at odds with his own childhood during which he was in danger every minute of his young life of being smothered with love by both of his parents.

"You don't have to marry me," she snuffled into his shirt.

"You're not getting away that easy," he said, taking her chin in his hand and kissing her softly on the mouth. Kate's revelation had only made him more determined to make sure that she had an abundance of love in her life for ever more.

"But I'll always be Joe Harrington's daughter. This will follow me around like a bad smell for the rest of my life," she argued.

"It will if you allow it to," he said, looking deep into her eyes. "Kate, you are an amazing woman. You are beautiful, kind and loyal. You are more than Joe Harrington's daughter. Do you hear me?"

"I wasn't kind to them," she said.

"You didn't know. Now that you do know, you can try to build some kind of relationship with your sisters. Your father is gone. Emer and Grace are still here. You never know, you might become like the Waltons because of this," said Jack, smiling.

Kate laughed at the thought of them all in a big bed with a hand-made quilt saying goodnight to all and sundry.

"OK, maybe not the Waltons," said Jack, "but there's nothing stopping you being friends. They did an amazing thing for you and you have all your life to do great things for them too."

Kate knew why she loved Jack. He was understanding and wonderful and she cried all over again at the thought of what her life would have been if he had decided he didn't want to marry her after all.

"So what are we going to tell the Food Network? Tell them it was all made up? Tell them some amateur reporter got the wrong end of the stick?" asked Jack.

Time was running out for them and they had to quash the rumours before they gained any more momentum.

"I'll do the radio interviews and if or when it comes up, I'll deny everything. Emer and Grace want that too. They don't want their dirty laundry aired in public any more than I do."

"Are you sure they won't bring it up again? You know, in a few years' time or something? When they're mad about something else you've done?" said Jack.

"Sorry – I didn't explain. That's not what happened. They didn't do it for spite. The reporter approached them – ambushed them really – they didn't approach her. And Grace blurted it out because she thought the reporter already knew, so she rushed in to say that I had never been abused."

"Trying to protect you again."

"Yes. So, it's done. It's between me and my sisters and that's where it's going to end. Besides, Emer doesn't want her daughter ever to know."

"Protecting her too then."

"Yes. And, Jack, I want you to meet them." And she kissed her handsome fiancé, feeling more loved and blessed than she deserved.

⁓⋙⋘⁓

Kate and Jack walked up the path that Kate had walked up the day before. The day before, she hadn't known anything. She had been secure in the knowledge that her sisters were wasters, taking after their waster, alcoholic father. She had been sure that she was just unlucky being born into the Harrington family at all. But now she knew she was lucky. Her sisters weren't wasters. They were survivors. Brave warrior sisters. Her father wasn't only a waster and an alcoholic, he was a child-abuser. A paedophile. God, she hated that word! It was strange but that word of all the words in the English language was the one that gave her chills. Even before she knew.

"Oh. Hi," said Emer when she opened the door. She stood back to let Kate and the gorgeous-looking guy in.

"Emer, this is Jack. My fiancé."

"Right. How'r'ya?" said Emer, hesitantly holding out her hand for Jack to shake.

"Go 'way out of that!" said Jack, leaning in. He hugged her and gave her a kiss on the cheek which actually made her blush to the top of her forehead.

"Who is it?" said Grace, coming out of the kitchen into the hallway.

"It's Kate – with Jack – her fiancé," said Emer dreamily, looking on enviously as Jack greeted Grace in the same way he did her.

"It's lovely to meet you both," said Jack.

Kate smiled at her gorgeous husband-to-be and couldn't help being amused at the effect he was having on her sisters.

"Tea?" asked Emer, keeping her sentence short, unable to trust her voice. It was hard to trust having happiness in their lives.

"Love some," said Jack and Kate in unison.

They moved into the kitchen and sat around Emer's kitchen table. Old hostilities seemed to thaw. Old disagreements and shouting matches were forgotten. Old barriers taken down.

When they were all drinking tea, Kate told them she wanted to ask them something.

"We told you," said Emer. "We're not going to say another thing about it. She wished she didn't have to repeat herself. She wished Kate believed that their secret was theirs to keep.

"No, it's not about the reporter. It's about our wedding," said Kate.

The two sisters looked at her, wondering what the hell that had to do with them.

"I want you to be my bridesmaids. And Kylie too. We want all of our family to be there."

Emer and Grace looked at her. The tough girls. The hardened women. They had tears in their eyes. They stood up and they hugged Kate. It was the first truly happy moment the three of them had ever shared.

# Chapter Fifty-Two

Tom and Molly walked along the beach, searching for pink seashells. It was as if a pink bomb had exploded in Tom's life. Molly had insisted on her room being painted the most lurid pink he had ever seen. The architect in him tried to resist the garish aesthetic but Molly insisted. And what Molly wanted, Molly got. She had been through too much for any just turned seven-year-old to have to go through.

Tom bent down to pick up a stone, only to discard it for not being pink enough. He watched as Molly and Ned ran along the shore with Ned chasing the breaking waves and barking like crazy.

"Daddy, can I go into the water with Ned? *Puhleaaase!*"

"No, it's too cold. You'll get pneumonia," said Tom.

"What's new nonia?"

"It's like the worst cold in the whole world. Do you remember when you had that nasty cough? And you had to take that black medicine? Yes? Well, pneumonia is a bazillion times worse than that."

Tom loved that he could exaggerate as much as he liked with Molly and that she believed every word he said.

It was such great fun being with a kid. He had spent such a long time being busy and never really getting to know his daughter that he was now making the most of every minute he had with her. She was amazing.

She missed her friends and often asked when she was going back to her 'real' school. The school where she was dressed like a nineteenth-century French enfant. She was enrolled in the local school in Inchahowen – the school Tom himself had attended and where his mother had taught. There, there was no uniform and she could wear anything she liked. Anything as long as it was pink. Honestly, Tom had never seen so much pink in his whole life. Emptying her wardrobe and drawers in Chelsea, he got his first introduction to the world of princesses, glitter and sparkle. Tom had wanted to leave some things behind, like glass slippers that looked like a death trap and some cheap nylon tat that looked like they had no place on a seven-year-old child. But these things happened to be Molly's very favourite items and into the suitcase and then into the wardrobe in Danny's old cottage they went.

"Oh! Will Ned get new nonia?"

"No. Dogs don't get pneumonia. They have special skin that doesn't feel the cold."

"Can I get special skin?"

"No, humans can't get special skin. We just have our own skin. You wouldn't like to be all hairy like Ned, would you?" Tom could see Molly considering it. Anything to get her into the waves. "I'll tell you what, Moll. We can get some wetsuits, you and me. Then we can go in the waves and we won't feel the cold."

Molly looked like she would burst with pure delight. "Now? Can we get them now? Please, Daddy, please!"

"Tomorrow. Now, come on. Call Ned. Tell him we're going home for dinner."

Ned had taken to following Molly everywhere she went. Not that Tom was complaining. Ned was making the transition from London to West Cork much easier for the little five-year-old. Tom tried to draw the line when Molly insisted that Ned be allowed to sleep at the foot of her bed but he gave up trying to persuade Ned to stay at the fire instead of curling up with his daughter.

"*Ned, it's dinnertime!*" she shouted, happily running after the little dog.

Tom was not a great cook and his lack of culinary expertise was not lost on Molly who insisted on eating only food that was coated in breadcrumbs or batter. Tom had enlisted the help of Mrs. Pierce who cooked wonderful meals for them.

Molly asked to be excused from the table.

"You didn't hardly eat anything!" said Tom, aghast at her almost full plate.

"I'm leaving it for Grandpa." This was a new excuse. It was normally that she was too full. Had a tummy ache. Felt sad. Felt sick.

"What do you mean?"

"You said that Grandpa is still here."

"I said that his spirit is still here. His spirit doesn't eat food so you can finish it yourself. Good girl."

Molly looked like she was being sent to the gallows but Tom couldn't give in on this one. He had caved on almost everything else. Wearing pink wellies with a tutu to school, even though he knew instinctively it was wrong. Having Ned sleep in her bed. Watching TV at breakfast. Combing the beach with her for shells instead of getting work done. The office in London almost forgot who he was, it had been so long since he'd actually contributed anything to the firm.

"I miss Kipper," she said sadly with a huge sigh.

Tom tried to work out who Kipper was. She had rattled off so many names in the past few months and he wasn't sure which ones were real and which ones were TV characters. Either way it was just another ploy to get out of eating the chicken and fresh vegetables.

"Which one is he again?"

"Daddy, I told you. He's my best friend in the whole world."

Ned whined and Molly laughed.

"Well, my second best friend in the whole world. He's my best friend in the United Kingdom. Ned's my best friend in Ireland. Anyhow, I miss him." She started to cry. Real tears.

Tom knew that dinner was gone out the window. Ned was already licking his lips, knowing that an organic breast of corn-fed chicken was coming his way.

"Oh, come on. We'll be visiting Mummy when she comes back to London for a visit soon and you'll see Kipper then. *Shhh ...*" he said, taking her on his knee and cuddling her.

So what if she ate chicken nuggets until she was eighteen? It wouldn't kill her surely?

# Chapter Fifty-Three

Tom turned off his computer and rubbed his eyes. It had been a long day. He had been up with Molly since six that morning. It was past nine o'clock and he was way behind where he should be as far as work was concerned. He knew that he must be testing the patience of his colleagues in the office in Canary Wharf. He consoled himself that it was one of the perks of being the majority owner that he wouldn't get fired for his lack of input.

He checked on Molly who was snoring softly in her pink bed. Ned wasn't at the end of the bed and Tom heard him clawing the front door to get out. Tom had already let him out to do his business and he was normally out for the count by now. He opened the front door again but Ned stood without moving.

Tom had no time for the dog's antics. He was tired and he wanted to go to bed himself. Ned scratched at the door and Tom opened it again.

"Get out, you silly mutt," he said to the dog but Ned didn't move.

Ned stared up at him and whined.

Tom wondered if something was wrong or if Ned was sick in some way. Animals had strange habits. If anything happened to the stupid dog Molly would lose her mind.

"What is it?" he asked the dog as he stepped out of the house with him.

Ned wagged his tail and started to walk towards the old cow path. Tom wondered where the bloody dog was going and turned on the flashlight on his phone and followed him.

Tom almost turned back around and went back home when he realised where Ned was headed. To Maud's house.

"No, Ned. Come on home," he said to the dog.

Ned duly ignorned him. The dog kept walking and was almost at Maud's front door. Tom had thought about Maud's house a lot since moving back to Inchahowen a week before. She still wasn't responding to his messages. He was certain that she wouldn't want to see him. Not after how badly he treated her.

"*Ned, come here!*" he said more forcefully.

But it was too late. Ned was not only scratching at Maud's door but had started to bark his head off. Tom launched himself at the door in an attempt to catch the dog by the scruff of the neck. Just as he got to the dog, he heard the door open. He looked up at Maud from his crouched position on her doorstep. He was stunned by her beauty as if seeing her for the first time.

"Ned, why are you making such a fuss?" she said, bending down to rub the dog on the head. She was at eye level with Tom.

"This fool of a dog had me chasing him across the field. I was following him trying to get him to come home. He normally sleeps at the end of Molly's bed. He's like her best friend in the world."

"I haven't seen him for a while," Maud said,

"Yes, Mrs. Pierce told me that he moved from her house to yours after Dad died. Thank you for taking care of him. To be honest, Ned was the last thing on my mind."

"It was nice to have the company. I thought he'd gone back to Mrs. Pierce's. I didn't know you were in town."

He stood and stared at her as she straightened up too. He wanted to take her in his arms and never stop kissing her but he had no right to do that. Not now.

"Molly? You said she's here? And your wife?" asked Maud, hoping against hope that he would respond in the negative.

"Just Molly. She lives with me now. Here. We both live here. It's so much better for her to grow up here than in London."

"But what about your, *em*, Valerie?"

"She's in Hong Kong. For work." Although Tom had his suspicions that Valerie and Hugo Bennett were doing more than working together.

"Oh. I see," Maud said, as though she didn't really see at all.

"Maud ... I'm sorry ... I treated you really badly. I was messed up. With Danny's funeral and other things ... I never told you any of it. I never got a chance ..."

"I know about the case. I read it in the paper."

"Look, Molly is asleep at home. I need to go back. Will you please come over? To Danny's? I want to talk to you, Maud. Properly. I need to talk to you. To be honest. Up front."

"Sure. But I'm in the middle of some paperwork. Give me half an hour to get organised."

"No problem. Come on, Ned."

Tom almost ran back to the house. Ned at his heels. This very ordinary day had taken a turn for the extraordinary. He started to tidy things around in the already neat house. He moved cushions, moved them back. Plumped them. Wiped already gleaming surfaces. Mrs. Pierce had the place shining as it was. There was very little he needed to do. He didn't know if he should tempt fate but he ran to his bedroom and pulled the sheets off his bed and replaced them with freshly laundered ones. He hoped he hadn't jinxed things. Now he prayed that Molly wouldn't wake up. Please, Molly, he urged his sleeping daughter. Let Daddy have some time with the nice lady.

Where the bloody hell was Ned? If Molly woke in the middle of the night and there was no sign of Ned, she would make straight for his room. And he fervently hoped that what would be going on his room later on would not be for a child's eyes. Bloody Ned. *Clever Ned* who had led him to Maud.

Tom changed his clothes and nearly killed himself when he fell over his feet that were stuck in the legs of his trousers. Get your act together, he ordered himself. Calm down. He sat on the side of his bed and took a deep breath. This was his one chance. To get her back. To tell her he was sorry. To beg for her forgiveness.

What was she doing? Was she going to open herself up to more hurt? Was she going to trust him again? Of course she was. She never hesitated for one moment. She pulled everything out of her suitcase until she found the dress. She took out the white floaty lace material which gained her tons of compliments whenever she wore it. She put it on with very little else, and sprayed perfume on her wrists. She put some on the back of her knees as well and laughed at the thought that he might smell it there.

Ready at last, she made her way to Tom's house and knocked softly at the door. She normally let herself in to Danny's but, now that it was Tom's house, she waited to be admitted. He opened the door and she walked in.

The place looked different. He had thrown out most of Danny's old furniture. The Formica table for one thing. The old dresser remained though. She noticed Danny's old chair in pride of place, at the stove.

"I see you've kept your dad's chair," she said approvingly.

"He loved that chair. When I was a kid, I remember him sitting in it, listening to his favourite radio programmes."

"While you and your mother sat at the table," she added.

"Yes. How did you know?"

"We stayed up drinking whiskey one night. It's a long story."

Tom raised an eyebrow at the thought of Maud and Danny tying one on.

"So what brought you back here? I thought hell would freeze over first," Maud said.

"I had an epiphany of sorts. After the court case. He wanted me to do something for the area. He loved Inchahowen almost as much as he loved me. I had to come back and put the wheels in motion."

"I have to admit I was pretty shocked when I heard about it first. I thought Danny would never want his land used for a hotel. But I now realise there was method in his madness. He wanted to ensure that there is a future for Inchahowen."

"The locals are mostly in favour. I just hope I can do justice with the design."

"No pressure then," she said and smiled. She was sure that he'd make Danny proud with whatever design he produced.

"Maud?"

"Yes?"

"I need to tell you something."

Maud caught the seriousness of his tone and waited, bracing herself for something unpleasant.

"I slept with Valerie. The night before the funeral."

Maud looked like she had been punched in the gut. He hated to hurt her but he had to come clean. He wanted to start afresh, start a new life with her and there could be no secrets.

"So it wasn't an act. At the funeral. I thought there had to be some mistake but the mistake was all mine. I thought you felt the same way I did. I thought you ..."

She turned to leave but then felt Tom's hand on her shoulder.

"Please, Maud. Wait. It was fucked up. I didn't want to do it but my emotions were all over the place. I was in my old house and my father had just died. She insisted on us sleeping in the same bed. I was exhausted and a bit drunk and just wanted to sleep. But then suddenly she was all over me. To be honest, I just wanted to get it over with."

"Oh please. Valerie's beautiful and she's the mother of your little girl. Don't insult me by saying you didn't want to have sex with her."

"But I didn't. I'm only telling you now because I don't want any secrets between us. I want to be with you for the rest of my life. If you'll have me, that is. I know I should have told her to get lost. I regret it, I do. There's nobody else I want to be with, Maud. For as long as we live."

# Chapter Fifty-Four

Kate stood in the porch of the church. Everyone was waiting for her. Jack was waiting at the altar. The music started up again and people began to shuffle in their seats.

"The natives are getting restless," Tom said.

"We have to wait for the bridesmaids. Where the fuck are they?" Kate said.

Tom shrugged. He hadn't laid eyes on Emer or Grace since arriving.

"Thanks for doing this by the way," she said. "It was either you or Doc or Haystack."

"*Eh*, well, I'll take that as a compliment. Anyway, it's my pleasure. It's not every day I get to walk a big celebrity down the aisle. You look beautiful, by the way."

"Did Maud tell you to say that?"

"Yes. Yes, she did. She warned me to say it, in fact. But you do. You look like a movie star."

And she did. After initially turning down stupid money from magazines vying for the wedding photos, she and Jack finally decided to take the money. But not for themselves. They were going to give the money to Emer and Grace.

"Christ! The organist is going to do his nut if we don't get going. Did you try calling them?"

"Hello?" she said, pointing to her fully regaled self. "Tell me where you'd put a phone in this get- up?"

"Fair point," he said.

Kate wasn't nervous. She was excited and thrilled at the prospect of marrying her best friend. Jack had been her rock and she had never known so much love and kindness from another human being. She had been very lucky. Charmed. It was like she had been lifted out of harm's way by invisible caring hands because it was deemed that hers would be a happy life full of love, friendship and success.

Kate heard the church doors open and immediately smelt cigarette smoke.

"*Jesus, will you get the fuck in here, please!*" she hissed. "*I'm trying to get married if it's not too much feckin' trouble!*"

"Jesus, calm down, would ya? We were only having a few puffs," said Grace as she began to fix the already perfect train of Kate's dress.

The smell of smoke swirled around them and Kate scrunched up her nose. Her sisters would never change. They smoked like chimneys, swore like troopers and Kate couldn't have loved them more.

Tom smiled at the exchange. They were like chalk and cheese, Kate and her sisters. The photographer was snapping away like mad and Tom imagined that people who bought the magazines would never know the shenanigans going on behind the beautiful scenes. At least they wouldn't smell the smoke.

"OK, no more cursing. That goes for you too, Kate," warned Tom as he took her arm and gave the nod to the usher to open the door. "Here we go!"

At the top of the aisle, after handing Kate over to Jack, Tom sat down in his place between Maud and Molly. He almost stepped on a furry paw and gave Molly a withering look. She had been warned not to bring Ned into the church.

"He came in by himself," she whispered.

He sort of believed her. She wouldn't mess this day up. She loved weddings and was dressed in the fluffiest, pinkest, most garish dress that Tom had ever seen.

"He did. Just appeared out of nowhere, didn't he, honey?" said Maud, patting Molly's hand reassuringly. The two had hit it off from the start. Maud didn't try to be anything that Molly didn't want her to be. She took it slowly and their love for each other blossomed organically. Molly was ready for a mother. And Maud was ready to love her.

Tom wished more than anything that it could have been him and Maud getting married. But Maud had insisted they wait. Until after the baby was born. She said she didn't want to get married looking like a beached whale. But she looked far from whale-like. In fact, Tom had never thought her more beautiful than she was right now, with her swollen belly, carrying the new life they made the night they reunited in Danny's old cottage.

### THE END

Printed in Great Britain
by Amazon

39561194R00173